Over-Experienced

BOOK TWO

karmen SCOTT

Contents

Disclaimer

✱ Note to readers: this story contains "*ebonics*".

According to Google, *ebonics* "is African American English, especially when viewed as a language in its own right rather than as a dialect of standard English."

*Contains some profanity.

*Contains fade-to-black scenes.

*Contains heavy Christian themes.

Author's Note

Dear reader,

Thank you so much for picking up this book. I am here in the year 2026 adding this note (to the revised and reformatted version) that I wish I would have known to add back when I started writing this in college. But when you come to know better, you do better.

So, before you dive into this story, I hope you have read the first book because this picks up after that one. Also, please keep in mind that this book, in particular, appears to be fast paced. However, I wrote this specific book as more of an outlet when I was dealing with depression before my diagnosis in college. And, honestly, this book may read that way.

However, this book also took me years to finish, even though it is technically short. I was dealing with a lot. But I hope beyond that, you can enjoy Kyrah's story and that you will continue to read on to the third book. (:

That said, happy reading! See you at the end!

Dedication

To my husband, DJ (Ashley):

Thank you for inspiring this story before there was a story. The story of Anthony and Kyrah was birthed and prophesied before I knew you. I remember I was writing this as we were getting close, and it clicked. You are my A. The real A&K. Thank you for believing in me. I love you.

Chapter One

It's a new year and I'm ecstatic to start it. After the year I had last year, I couldn't hold my excitement to start fresh. I changed up my look a little by adding blonde highlights to my hair and getting a nose piercing. I wanted to spice up my look and do something different. It was a plus that Jesse liked it, too. He and I have been together for about four months now and truthfully, it was rough not being able to see him all the time. And honestly, things have felt a little off between us lately, but I just brushed it off and figured it was because of the distance between us. So, since we both moved back to campus the same day, we decided to spend the evening together to make up for lost time.

"Babe, you ready? I got us reservations for 7 and we gon' be late at the rate you goin'", Jesse said as he walked into my room while looking at his phone.

I rolled my eyes, "Almost. I can't find my gold hoops, though." I searched for them until I finally found them. I looked at Jesse as I put them on.

"Um, can you look up from your phone and tell me how I look?" I asked sarcastically. He glanced at me and did a double-take. He smiled and walked towards me.

"You look perfect."

I blushed, "Thanks, boo." I grabbed my phone and purse, and we walked out hand-in-hand. Since Tamra and Raynah hadn't moved in yet, Jesse decided it would be perfect to take me on a date before they got a hold of me.

The drive to the restaurant was about thirty minutes so we got there at a pretty decent time. The hostess guided us to our table for two and I must say, this place was pretty prestigious. Jesse outdid himself with this one.

We sat down and looked over our menus in silence until our waitress came and took our drink and appetizer orders. After she walked away, I looked at my phone. I blushed feeling Jesse's stare.

"Can I have my face back?" I asked finally looking at him.

He smirked, "My bad. I can't help it, though. You look so beautiful."

I smiled, "You're so sweet. Thank you." He smiled and nodded. We talked for a little while longer before our waitress came back with our drinks.

It was so nice to spend time with Jesse. Although we saw each other a few times during the summer, it was sporadic. I missed him and it had only been two full months. Plus, he works so much that we didn't talk as much as I would have liked, but when we could, we definitely did.

We stayed at the restaurant for about two hours until we decided to leave. He didn't want us to go back to the school just yet, so we just drove around until we ended up in an empty parking lot with a nice view of the night sky.

"Did you enjoy dinner?" he asked me as he put the car in park and reclined his seat a little bit. I reclined mine and rested my head on the seat.

I nodded, "I did. It was good. I got the itis now."

He laughed, "Me, too, man. I could go to sleep right here." I laughed with him and sighed. We sat in silence for a minute.

"I really missed you."

I smiled, "I missed you, too."

He grabbed my hand and intertwined our fingers. He kissed the back of my hand and stared into my eyes. The look in his eyes was so captivating. As much as I wanted to look away, I couldn't. His stare quickly turned into a lustful one and he smirked. *Oh, Lord... I know that look...* He leaned over and kissed me slowly. I eagerly kissed him back as he moved closer to me. He pushed his seat back further and pulled me on top of his lap. He kissed my neck, and I closed my eyes...

Kyrah... Kyrah... I suddenly heard the Holy Spirit again. We started kissing passionately, and although I knew it was going downhill from here, I started to really get into it without thinking twice about it. I could feel my heart breaking. I could feel God's disappointment and we hadn't even gone that far.

Anthony moved from my lips back to my neck. I closed my eyes suddenly feeling like I was in complete bliss. Why does this feel so good? He stopped all of a sudden. I slowly opened my eyes to meet his, full of lust.

He smirked, "You wanna stop?" His voice was abnormally deeper. I liked it. No, I loved it. Of course, my spirit wants to

stop... But physically, I can't. I bit my bottom lip slightly as I shook my head "No".

He nodded, "A'ight. Let's go to my room." I got off his lap as he grabbed a hold of one of my hands. He led me to his room and closed the door. After he locked it, he sat on the bed with his eyes still on me. He grabbed my hand and slowly pulled me closer to stand between his legs.

"You sure you wanna do this?" he asked sincerely. I nodded too fast. I didn't even think about it. He smirked as he leaned in to kiss me. Now I knew there was no turning back...

Anthony? I quickly opened my eyes and gently pushed Jesse away. I went against my flesh, as much as I wanted us to keep going. He looked at me and frowned with eyes full of lust, but quickly softened his face when he realized what was happening.

"Maybe we shouldn't... You know... Not how I wanna start off the year," I said as I slowly got off his lap and back into the passenger seat. He rolled his eyes and rested his head on the headrest.

"Kyrah, come on, man... You killin' me with this...", he responded a little low.

I frowned, "Jesse, you know already know how I feel about this." I looked down at my lap feeling slightly guilty for thinking about Anthony.

"I know, but you can't keep teasin' me... That's not cool, bruh." I nodded in agreement wanting this conversation to be over.

"Okay, Jesse..."

We drove back to school in awkward silence. Our date night took a wrong turn very fast. He walked me to my room and stood in the hallway, but we wouldn't look at each other.

I rolled my eyes, "Jesse—"

He nodded, "No... I'm sorry for what I said in the car. I should've kept my cool. My fault." He looked down and shoved his hands in his pockets. I frowned and stared at him.

"I mean, it's fine, but can you at least look at me?"

"Nah. You look too good to me right now and if I look at you, I'ma take you in the room and give you the business." I burst out laughing. I hit him on the arm, and he finally looked at me and laughed. He grabbed my hand and pulled me closer to him and frowned a little bit.

"I am sorry, for real," he said.

I smiled and reached up to touch his face.

"It's okay. I appreciate that. I don't think we should be alone like that anymore. It'll just be easier for both of us."

He nodded hesitantly agreeing, "Yeah, I guess... Well, I'ma go to my room and go to sleep. I gotta work in the morning." I nodded and hugged him.

"See you later," he said before giving me a kiss.

I smiled as we parted, "Okay, goodnight."

"Night." I went inside my suite, and he walked away. I went to my room at the end of the hallway and sat on my bed. I stared straight ahead recalling everything that happened and what would've happened in that parking lot. *This is not how I pictured my first night back...* Suddenly, I started feeling guilty for two different reasons. The first reason is that I almost had sex with Jesse, which shouldn't have even happened in the first place; the second reason is for allowing thoughts of Anthony to creep into my mind. I hadn't seen nor talked to Anthony since we moved out last semester, so why am I thinking about him?

Honestly, I did wonder how he had been doing and what he'd been up to, but I would quickly shake those thoughts. I wasn't even sure if he was coming back. I seemed to have wiped Anthony completely out of my radar because he no longer held an important position in my life.

I shook my head and distracted myself by turning on my TV. I changed into my pajamas, lay comfortably in my bed, and watched a show on Netflix. Catching me off guard, my phone vibrated repeatedly. Debating on whether I wanted to talk to anybody or not, I decided against it and put my phone on silent. I watched the show until I dozed off into a deep sleep...

Chapter Two

I woke up the next morning to the sound of Tamra and Raynah banging on my door. As much as I wanted to be upset at them for interrupting my sleep, I was excited to see them. I quickly got out of bed and ran to open the door. We all squealed and hugged once we saw each other.

"I have missed you guys so much!" I exclaimed still hugging them.

"We missed you, too, girl! This has been the longest summer ever," Tamra said as we all parted from our group hug. It was difficult living in a completely different city while everybody else stayed here. Considering we weren't able to go on the trip we originally planned, I was only able to see Tamra and Raynah once during the summer, and it was only for a day.

"What are we gettin' into today, shawties?" Raynah asked with a huge smile plastered on her face.

"I was thinking we go get some lunch then go see a movie," Tamra suggested. I nodded and shrugged. Anything sounded good as long as we could hang out. They left my room so I could get ready for the day. I took a nice hot shower, brushed my teeth, and washed my face. I applied very light makeup, which barely looked like I had any on besides my lip gloss. I took my headscarf off just as Tamra walked out of her room. She gasped and gave me a goofy smile.

"Your hair!!! When did you do this? It wasn't like this when we hung out this summer."

I laughed, "I did it the day before I came back. I wanted to make a drastic change."

She nodded, "It's definitely you. I love it. What does Jesse think?"

I shrugged, "He really likes it." She smiled and nodded.

We talked and caught up a little the whole time I was getting ready. I was done within the next fifteen minutes. I shot Jesse a quick text telling him I was going out with Tamra and Raynah. He didn't respond so I just shrugged it off. We ended up going to a sushi shop close by. The waitress seated us as soon as we walked in.

"So, missy, what's up?" Raynah asked me while we were looking over our menus.

I debated on if I wanted to tell them about what almost happened last night. Eventually, it would come up, so I decided against it.

"Nothing much. Just been ready to get back in school."

She nodded, "Yeah, I feel you. I need a break from Tommy. I love him, but he has been in my face all break." Tamra and I laughed at her complaint.

"You always bring him up in the most unnecessary times," Tamra stated still laughing. Raynah laughed and shrugged.

"Sorry."

I smiled, "Don't apologize. It's funny."

We stayed at the restaurant for about two hours talking and laughing and ended up missing the movie. By the time we arrived back at school, we were all tired and ready to just relax. I lay in bed and watched a movie until my phone started lighting up from a phone call. **BABE** my phone read and a picture of me and Jesse appeared on the screen.

"Hello?" I answered sleepily.

"You sleep?" he asked loudly through the phone.

"Why are you so loud? And no, I'm not. I'm watching a movie in my room."

"My bad. Okay, well, I'm outside so come open the door."

"Alright." I hit the end option on my phone and got out of bed with my blanket wrapped around me like a cocoon. I went to the main door of the suite and opened it to see Jesse staring at me with a straight face.

"Fix your face", I stated as I started to walk back to my room. He laughed as he followed me into my room.

"Dang. You so rude. First, you hang up in my face and now you tellin' me what to do," he joked. I rolled my eyes, not really in the mood to joke around with him. I lay back down in a fetal position, and he positioned himself behind me. I honestly felt in my Spirit that he shouldn't even be here laying like this with me, but going against my better judgment, I ignored the feeling.

"How was your day?" he asked.

"It was fun. We went to eat and missed our movie because we lost track of time at the restaurant."

He chuckled, "Y'all talk too much." I frowned and turned around to face him.

"We really don't." My response came off with a little more attitude than I expected, but I guess it was just spilling over from the day.

He sighed. "What's up with you, man?"

"Did you see my message earlier?" I quickly responded. He face-palmed and looked at me.

"My bad. I saw it but I forgot to respond." Confusion spread across my face as I tried to make sense of what he'd just said.

"Um okay... well what were you doing that makes you forget to respond to your girlfriend?" I tried to lighten it up with a slight chuckle to hide my irritation, but I couldn't. Something just wasn't right. He frowned a little bit returning the chuckle.

"Baby, why are you checking me? I said sorry."

"I'm not checking you... I was just asking a question but forget it." I shook my head and turned my attention to my phone. I started scrolling on Instagram to distract my brain. Something was off but I decided to just trust Jesse because he was my boyfriend. If he said he forgot, then he forgot. What could I do about it? While I was busy scrolling on my phone, I felt Jesse move closer to me trying to get my attention.

"What, Jesse?" I asked annoyed.

"You know you look so cute when you're upset. You expect me to take you seriously while you're wrapped up in this big behind blanket like a big baby, but I can't."

I rolled my eyes and pouted, "Whatever." He smiled and leaned in to kiss me. I moved my head which made him laugh. He kept trying to kiss me, but I kept dodging him.

He smacked his lips, "Man, stop playin'. I ain't kissed you all day. I want a kiss." He leaned in to kiss me again and I dodged his lips. He rolled his eyes and smacked his lips. At first, I was doing it maliciously but now I was doing it because it was funny to mess with him. Before I knew it, I felt him tickling me making me scream and laugh harder. As much as I wanted to tell him to stop, I didn't have the energy to because I was laughing too much.

After two minutes of being tickled, he ended up on top of me with my arms pinned above me. I stared at him trying to catch my breath.

"You know I hate being tickled," I said still laughing a little.

He smirked, "I know. That's why I did it." I smiled. He leaned down and finally kissed me. We kissed innocently for a while, but eventually, he deepened the kiss. I was almost starting to feel like fighting him off was hopeless at this point. What almost happened in the car was literally about to happen in my bed. I had finally gotten to a point where I had forgiven myself for what I did last year when I gave myself away before marriage, but here I was with Jesse about to do the same thing. Instead of fighting him off and pushing him away, I just went with it and completely ignored the Holy Spirit, who I'm pretty sure is over me at this point.

"Jesse…" I said softly as he moved his lips to my neck.

"Hmm?" he responded lowly still kissing me. I sighed wondering if I should say something or not. I wanted him as badly as I wanted to tell him to stop. He finally looked at me with lust-filled eyes.

"You good?" he asked in a deeper voice. Forgetting what I was even going to say, I nodded. Things escalated quickly and eventually, both of us were just in our underwear. Just as things were about to go further, someone knocked on my door. *Seriously?*

Jesse grunted, "Ignore it."

"Kyrah," I heard Tamra say from outside the door. Jesse smacked his lips, slowly getting off me. I slipped on my robe and cracked the door a little. I silently prayed and thanked God for stopping it when he did.

"Yes ma'am?" I said looking at Tamra nervously. She smiled at me, clearly oblivious to what was about to happen behind this door.

"I made reservations for the crew tonight at that new Mexican restaurant nearby. I sent a group text to everybody to be ready by 7:00." I smiled and nodded.

"Okay, sounds good. I'll be ready by then." She nodded and walked away, disappearing into her room. I closed the door and stared at Jesse who was staring back at me.

"Jesse, we can't keep doing this..." I finally said after moments of us just looking at each other. His face read that he didn't understand what I was talking about.

I sighed and stared at him noticing that he was still in his boxers. He looked appealing, especially with his locs hanging loosely. After gathering my thoughts and stopping myself from staring at him, I took a deep breath.

"We can't keep teasing each other by being alone, almost going all the way, then stopping once we realize what's happening."

He sighed, "Here we go..."

I rolled my eyes, "Jesse, please don't start."

"You know what," he began, "Honestly, I don't think I can do this..."

I frowned, "What are you talking about?"

"This, Kyrah. Us... It's just not workin'." I froze unable to think of the words to say to respond. What had changed from four months ago when he wanted to be with me so badly? When he said he saw a future with me? Maybe Sean was right, and I had fallen for the trap of a handsome face and charming words once again. Tears formed in my eyes and as much as I tried to swallow them away, I couldn't.

"Kyrah, I'm sorry. I really am. I know I said I wanted to wife you and all'at, and trust me, I meant it. But maybe... We need to take some time apart. You know... this is hard for me. And I really do care about you, but—"

I frowned, "Jesse, where is all this coming from? Are you breaking up with me?" He continued to look down and shrugged. He finally looked at me with sad eyes. I shook my head in disbelief.

"Wow. Well, okay. If this is what you want to do, then fine." He got up and walked towards me, but I backed up.

"Kyrah, listen—"

"Can you please just get your stuff and leave?" I tried to fight back the tears that threatened to fall from my eyes, but I couldn't. He tried to talk to me, but I heard nothing he said. All I knew was I was heartbroken once again. He finally gave up, so he put his clothes on, grabbed his things, and left. I sat on my bed feeling empty. The tears I tried to hold in all came out at once, leaving me feeling completely hopeless.

All I could think was why God would allow this to happen to me a second time in a year. *Why me, God? What am I doing wrong? I thought you forgave me... I stopped it before anything happened!* I kept crying until I saw Tamra standing in my doorway.

"Are you okay?" she asked as she walked in and sat beside me. I tried to gather myself together, but that only made me cry more. "What happened? I saw Jesse leave. He looked upset. I didn't even know he was here," she continued.

I sighed, "I don't wanna talk about it right now. I'm gonna get ready for dinner." She looked at me sincerely but just nodded. Once she left my room, I got myself together. I knew I had to put on a smile at this dinner just to avoid more questions besides "Where is Jesse?" since I'm sure he's not coming.

I took a quick shower, changed my makeup from daytime to evening then picked out my outfit. I settled for a fitted black dress that went right below the knees with spaghetti straps and some white converses. I figured I might as well look the exact opposite of how I felt so no one would know how heartbroken I was. Just as I was doing one last outfit check in the mirror, Tamra came in and told me we were about to leave. I nodded. Exhaling slowly, I grabbed my belongings and followed Tamra and Raynah out of my room. They were in deep conversation while I was in deep thought.

I thought everything was going great. How could he do this to me? Had he been wanting to break up with me? What did I do wrong? God, what did I do? Do You want me to be single forever? Two guys have become exes all in the course of one year. Maybe I should talk to him and see what I can-

"Kyrah" Raynah said pulling me out of my sad thoughts. I turned my attention to her with glistening eyes, trying to keep from crying. "Are you okay?" she asked. I looked around and noticed we were in the car already riding to whatever restaurant we were going to. I had been so caught up in my brain, I hadn't realized we had left.

"Yeah, I'm okay", I finally responded. She nodded and turned her attention back to Tamra. They continued their conversation, and I continued questioning everything that just took place in my room in my head. *Everything seems to be falling apart...*

Chapter Three

D ays passed, classes started, and here I was still trying to figure out where things went wrong. Jesse hadn't returned any of my calls nor had he texted me back. He was all around ignoring me and going on with his life. What was supposed to be the beginning of something great and an amazing year turned out to be the exact opposite. I tried talking to God about it and expressing to Him how I felt, but I always ended up angry and not wanting to talk to Him anymore.

It was the last day of class for the first week of school and I was walking back to my room when I saw a familiar figure walking towards me. I squinted my eyes knowing exactly who it was.

"Hey, Kyrah!" the voice of the familiar person said. I put on a fake smile, not because I had an issue with her, but because I didn't want to look like I was sad, even though I clearly was.

"Hey, Erica. How have you been?"

She smiled, "I've been great. How about you?"

Miserable. "Same. Just happy to be back at school." *I'd rather be somewhere in a hole.* She smiled a little and nodded.

"Well, I gotta get to class, but it's good seeing you. We should grab lunch soon!" I actually smiled a genuine smile. Never would I have imagined ever being cool with Erica, but I'm glad we are.

"Yeah, definitely! I'll give you my number so we can plan it." We exchanged numbers and went our separate ways. As soon as I got to my room, the wave of sadness took over. With it only being the first week of school, I had no homework, so I just lay in my bed and stared at the ceiling. I knew I needed to talk to someone about what I was feeling and dealing with, but I didn't want to put all my problems on someone else.

To some people, this might not seem like a big deal, but after the year I've experienced this hurt. Plus, I didn't feel like being judged because I'd been with two guys in a short period of time. I lay there and cried silent tears. I thought about reaching out to Jesse again but decided against it after a long debate in my head. He obviously didn't want to talk to me if he hadn't even tried to respond after all this time. Surprisingly, Tamra and Raynah hadn't asked me about him, but I'm guessing it's because they figured I would tell them when and if I wanted to. As of right now, talking about it is not an option.

Just as I was about to drift off into sleep after crying for about thirty minutes, my phone rang. I looked to see who it was, although I had no intention of answering it right now. A frown grew on my face when I didn't recognize the number. It looked familiar but I didn't care enough to answer and see who it was, so I just let it ring. After the call ended, I received a voicemail shortly after. I was not in the mood to talk to anybody, so I left it alone. Within minutes, I drifted into a deep sleep...

"Okay, Kyrah. We have let you mope and be sad for almost a week now. But you gotta talk to us. What's going on with you?" Raynah asked. I was surprised by the tone of her voice. Normally Tamra is the one to ask me questions, but not this time. I looked at Tamra, and she was looking at me waiting for me to answer. They both stared at me with concern. I sighed trying not to cry in front of everybody in the cafeteria.

"Jesse and I broke up. He broke up with me..." Their mouths both formed into a small "o".

"Why?? What happened?" Tamra asked. *I guess now is the time to tell them...*

"We almost slipped twice, last Friday night after our date and last Saturday. So, I told him that we should just chill. Like, we don't need to be alone anymore so both of us won't slip and he basically said that was too hard for him, so he broke up with me. I've tried to call him and text him, but he won't respond to me. I don't know what to do."

Raynah sighed, "Well, I didn't see that coming."

"Me neither. I thought you guys just got into an argument or something. I didn't know it was that serious", Tamra chimed in.

"Yeah, well... I didn't really expect it either. I thought everything was good between us. He was acting a little distant when we got back, but I didn't think anything of it."

"You think he was cheating?" Raynah asked. Tamra frowned and waited for me to answer.

"I tried not to think like that, but I don't know what to think anymore."

Tamra shook her head and looked around. "We gon' find out. He can't do that to you."

I chuckled, "Chill. It's whatever. I'll be fine, I promise."

After we left the cafeteria, I decided to go sit in the coffee shop on campus just to take my mind off things. I took one of my favorite books and sat in a booth to read. This was my favorite thing to do when I felt down or needed to stop thinking for a while. Twenty minutes passed and I was absorbed in the book. So deep that I didn't even hear someone calling my name.

"Kyyyyyraaahhhh" I heard the familiar, deep voice say. I looked up from my book with a blank expression. Butterflies instantly started flying around in my stomach when I laid eyes on the person standing before me. *Anthony.* He chuckled and sat in the seat across from me.

"You good? You deep in that book, I see."

I laughed a little, "Yeah, I am. Sorry. I didn't hear you calling my name." He smiled.

"It's cool. How are you? I tried calling you earlier." *He did? Oh! That's who that was.*

"Oh, yeah. I was asleep, and never got a chance to call back. Sorry again." *It's not a complete lie.*

"Nah, I figured you've been busy. You're a busybody", he laughed, "But it's so good to see you. You look beautiful as always." My heartbeat quickened and my palms started sweating. I smiled and looked down at my lap. Once I looked back up at him, I caught myself staring. *He looks so handsome. His locs are longer and so neat. Bruh... He's even finer than before.*

"Thank you. It's good to see you, too", I finally responded. He smirked and bit his bottom lip, slightly. He stood up and I found myself getting a little disappointed.

"I gotta go to class, but I'll see you around...?"

I nodded, "Yeah, of course." He smiled and nodded.

"Cool, cool. Later, Kyrah." I waved and watched him walk away.

Being with him for a few minutes made me miss him so much. But relationships are not my thing, apparently. I canceled out any resurfacing feelings for him and tried to keep reading my book. I couldn't allow Anthony back into my life, boyfriend-wise, simply because I knew it wouldn't last. Not now, at least. Breaking up with Jesse was starting to turn into a wake-up call. Something in my life had to change, I'm just not sure what that is exactly.

After trying to refocus on the book for a whole thirty minutes, I gave up and decided to go back to my room. The walk was short since I was too wrapped up in my head to even pay attention to everything around me. I walked into my suite and was face to face with Raynah's boyfriend, Tommy.

"Wassup, Kyrah?" he asked enthusiastically. I gave a small smile.

"Hey, Tommy. Not much."

"Tommy, get out of her face", Raynah said annoyed. I fake laughed and walked past him to get to my room. Mistakenly, I left my room door open, so I was able to hear their conversation.

"Yo, we should double date with her and ole boy. What's his name? Jonathan? Jermaine?" Tommy said. As much as I wanted to laugh at him getting Jesse's name wrong, I couldn't. All I could do was feel sad.

"Jesse, and no. That's not going to happen", Raynah responded, sounding even more annoyed.

"Why not?"

"Don't worry about it, Tommy." I couldn't take it anymore. I got up from my bed, closed the door, and locked it. Tears formed in my eyes, and I knew I couldn't stop them. I stared at myself in the mirror hanging on my closet door. *This cannot be my life... There has to be more to life than this... I'm losing myself.*

The rest of the night was filled with more tears, feeling sorry for myself, and fighting the urge to reach out to Jesse. I fell asleep after that non-activity at around one in the morning. When I woke up the next morning, I could feel how puffy my eyes were. I had mixed emotions. Old feelings resurfaced from seeing Anthony after not talking to him for three months, and pain from my most recent heartbreak. While everybody else on campus was out enjoying their Saturday and planning to go out and party, I had no desire to do any of that. All I wanted to do was lay in bed, eat ice cream, and watch sad movies all day. There was nothing that could make me feel better at this point. Talking to God was completely out of the question currently, simply because I wasn't in the mood for "I told you so's". I genuinely felt like He was over me nowadays to even want to fool with my sob story. That seemed to be the only explanation I could think of for why He let my relationship fall apart. Like I said, relationships just don't seem to be my thing. Even my relationship with Him seemed to be falling apart...

Chapter Four

More weeks have passed and things were still the same. Besides doing my schoolwork, I've been doing nothing but moping. I honestly wanted to get out of this funk, but I just couldn't. And this point, it wasn't even about Jesse anymore. It was more so about me trying to figure out what was wrong with me. I was having a hard time getting past the fact that everything went completely left so fast. My daily routine was going to class and going back to my room, maybe going to get some food in between. Not to mention, I've lost a little weight, and it was definitely obvious. Tamra and Raynah would express their concern, but I just brushed it off.

It's currently Thursday night and it's raining. I'm lying in the dark listening to myself breathe. Knowing I had some work to do, I decided against it. It wasn't due for another week, but I normally like to go ahead and get it out of the way. Lately, this has been a nightly routine for me. The only difference with this night was the fact that I couldn't seem to fall asleep. For the past couple of days, I've been replaying my breakup in my head. I looked at the clock on my desk and it read 9:00

p.m. I sighed and pulled the blanket over my head. I think it was safe to say I was walking into depression if I hadn't already......... *Nah. I'm not depressed. I'll be okay...*

There was a soft knock on my door that startled me. I didn't want to talk to anyone, so I just ignored it and acted like I was asleep. No one could understand the way I was feeling at that moment, so I killed the idea of talking to anyone. I heard whoever was trying to open the door but gave up and continued to knock once they realized it was locked.

"Did she answer?" I heard a male voice ask. *Ugh. I want nothing to do with the male population.*

"No, she's been in her room for weeks, besides going to class. She barely eats. I don't know what to do. I'm worried about her," I heard Tamra faintly say. A tear managed to slip from my eye. Sadness washed over me. I was over feeling like this, but I had no idea how to get out of it.

"Okay, let me try," I heard the male voice say. *Please don't.*

"Okay, thanks, Anthony." *Oh, God.* Then there was a knock. Not as soft, but familiar.

"Kyrah, please open the door. Come on." I sobbed silently not knowing why I was crying in the first place. After listening to him knock for a whole sixty seconds, I knew he wasn't giving up, so I gave in and opened the door. I know I looked crazy, but I didn't care. Tears kept falling from my eyes as we stood there looking at each other.

"Can I come in?" he asked. I saw Tamra standing there with a relieved expression since I opened the door.

"Why did you call him?" I asked her, completely ignoring his question.

She sighed, "I didn't. I ran into him earlier and he asked about you because he hadn't seen you in around in a while. I was desperate. Kyrah, you don't come out of that room. It's been weeks, and you're not eating. I'm worried." I wiped the tears that kept escaping my eyes and looked down at my feet.

"I'm fine" was all I could manage to say.

"Kyrah—" Tamra started to say but Anthony stopped her, giving her a reassuring look.

She looked at me with a worried expression and hesitantly nodded. She went to her room and left her door cracked. He looked down at me and I looked up at him. On cue, tears rolled down my face.

"Let's go for a ride. I'll wait here while you put some clothes on."

I shook my head, "I don't want to. I just want to go to sleep." He looked at me with sad eyes.

"Kyrah... Please." This was a softer side of Anthony I'd never seen. I had a massive war going on in my head on whether I should go with him or not. I really didn't feel like it, but I didn't feel like doing anything these days.

"Please..." he said one last time. I reluctantly nodded and went back into my room to change clothes. All I did was toss on some joggers, a hoodie, and my Nike slides. I grabbed my phone and keys and followed him out of my room silently. He peeked into Tamra's room to let her know we were leaving, and I followed him out the door.

The first ten minutes of the ride were completely quiet. He didn't have any music playing. I was starting to think that this was pointless until he broke the silence.

"What's going on with you? You didn't seem like anything was going on when I saw you a few weeks back." I stayed silent simply because I knew if I talked, I would cry. Crying was starting to become a nuisance for me.

"You gotta talk to someone. Even if it's not me or Tamra or who-ever. You can't stay like this."

"I'm okay. I promise" I tried to convince him and myself that I was fine, even though I knew that wasn't true. He took a deep breath and kept driving. Another twenty passed and we were still riding around. It was now 10:15. Honestly, I was enjoying this quiet ride. After staring out the window, I looked at Anthony.

"Jesse broke up with me when we got back to school," I blurted out fighting back the tears that sat in my throat. He nodded as if to tell me to keep talking. "I don't know why. I haven't seen him. I tried to reach him, but he hasn't returned any calls or texts. He just completely stopped talking to me. I don't know what to do... And I think what's hurting me the most is that I'm letting it get to me so much that I'm questioning myself, my morals, everything. And now... I can't seem to shake this."

Waterworks. Instantly. Tears continuously flowed from my already tired eyes. I shook my head looking down at my hands in my lap. It felt good to just talk, although I had been avoiding it. Keeping it all in seemed to be the right thing to do, but I was wrong. Releasing felt better. Anthony reached over with his free hand and grabbed one of my hands. He rubbed the back of it with his thumb. I sighed and looked out of the window...

We got back to the school around 11:00 and it was very quiet on campus since a lot of people were out partying. He walked me back to my room and sat with me in the living room for a few minutes. He looked at me and I looked back at him. Totally misreading the situation, I leaned in a little and he backed up. He gave me a sad smile.

"Kyrah, you don't wanna do this." *What just happened...?* "You're just feeling vulnerable. I don't want to take advantage of you while you're like this." I nodded in understanding and looked away.

"I think you should talk to someone. I can call my pastor and see if his wife would be willing to talk to you. They're really cool." I frowned and looked at him. *Pastor? When did he start going to church?*

"I don't need to talk to anyone. I'm fine. I'm not depressed." He looked at me concerned.

"The fact that you have to try to convince me says that you should at least consider it. I'll go with you if you're not comfortable going alone." I rolled my eyes, "I'm fine, Anthony. I don't need to talk to anyone. I'll be okay. I'll get over this eventually."

"Kyrah, you're unintentionally losing weight because you barely eat. You're walking around here like a zombie or a robot. We're all concerned about you. You need to talk to someone. I'm not gonna sit here and watch you kill yourself."

"Then don't." I looked away from him and folded my arms. I didn't mean to sound so harsh, but I genuinely didn't feel like I needed any kind of counselor. He sighed.

"I'll call them anyway. I'm not giving up; I hope you know that. I'll come by and check on you tomorrow, okay?" He stood up and I looked at him.

"Okay..." He leaned down and kissed me on the forehead. I closed my eyes and a tear escaped. "You'll get through this", he encouraged. I watched as he walked out of the door, and I just sat there...

The next day came pretty fast and just as Anthony promised, he came to check on me. We were sitting in the living room waiting for his pastor to answer his phone. After three rings, a deep voice came through the speaker.

"Hello?"

"Hey, Pastor Kendrick, this is Anthony."

"Hey, man! How's it going?"

"Everything's going great..." He kept talking and I zoned out the rest of their conversation. I had no interest in talking to a stranger about my problems. For what? It wouldn't solve anything. What could a stranger possibly tell me about _myself?_ I rolled my eyes at the thought. Already annoyed, I looked at Anthony who was laughing at something his pastor said. I admired his side profile. *Why did we even break up? He was the best thing that ever happened to me. Sure, he had issues, but who doesn't? And when the heck did he start going to church??*

"Alright, Kyrah", he began pulling me out of my thoughts, "He said not to pressure you, but if you want, his wife would love to meet with you tomorrow at noon."

I sighed, "Anthony, I appreciate all this, but I don't really feel like it's that serious."

He nodded, "I know. But it is to me, Tamra, and Raynah. And you know how much I love... Care about you. I just want you to be okay. After Tamra told me about how you've been stuck in your room, crying all the time, and barely eating, I got worried. I walked over here as fast as I could. She told me Jesse wasn't an option and nonexistent to her right now," he chuckled, "but I knew I had to be here. Even if I was the last person you wanted to talk to about this..."

He stared at me and saw the look on my face. Hearing that name stung. Tears threatened to escape my eyes, but I did my best to swallow them away. I was contemplating whether or not to go talk with this stranger, but I just stayed silent and looked at him with hopeless eyes. He gave a small, sad smile.

"Just think about it, at least. I'm not pressuring you, but I will go with you if you want me to." I looked down at my lap and nodded.

"I'll think about it. I promise."

Chapter Five

"**K**yrah, you don't have to do this if you want to." I looked away from the window and looked at Anthony. I sighed.

"It's okay. I'm already here so might as well try, I guess." He smiled and nodded. He opened the driver-side door and then looked at me. The words "Don't open the door" escaped his lips and I chuckled. I sat patiently and waited for him to come to my side and open my door.

We walked inside the church, and I looked around. I tried not to be annoyed, or at least not show it since I did agree to come. No one forced me to. As we were walking down the hall, I noticed how small the church was. *This is a lot tinier than I expected.* Anthony led me to the pastor's office, and we were greeted by the secretary.

"Anthony how are you?" She greeted a little too cheerfully for me.

A big grin appeared on his face, "I'm good, Sasha. How about you?" Once again, I zoned him out. I don't know what it is about him these days, but he's a completely different person. He started going to church, stopped sagging his pants, and his whole demeanor was different. Part of me was okay with it, but the other part of me was annoyed at the fact that he was helping *me* and not the other way around.

"Kyrah," Anthony pulled me out of my thoughts, grabbing my hand, "You okay? You kinda zoned out." I put on a fake smile and nodded.

"Yeah, I'm fine. I was just admiring the church."

He nodded, "Oh okay. Well, come on. She's waiting for us." I nervously nodded and followed him to the first lady's office. I looked down and noticed that Anthony was still holding my hand as if he was letting me know he wasn't going anywhere. My heart ached and smiled at the same time because I knew we could never be what we once were again.

We walked into a cute office and were greeted by a very young-looking, gorgeous, brown-skinned woman. She looked to be about thirty or so, but I didn't want to stare too long. She looked at me and smiled.

"You must be Kyrah." I nodded. "Nice to meet you, I'm Moriah. [*So casual.*] You're right Anthony, she's gorgeous." I looked at Anthony, who was already staring at me and smiling. She invited us to sit down across from her and make ourselves comfortable.

"So, Kyrah, talk to me. Tell me about yourself." I had no idea what to say. Every bit of information about myself left about three to four weeks ago. I just looked at her searching for words to say.

"I don't know who I am anymore, so I can't." She nodded with sympathy on her face.

"Okay, and why do you think that is?" I shrugged and looked around. A tear escaped my eye, and I looked down at my lap. "Kyrah, I don't expect you to open up right away. Your silence is normal and anticipated. But I do hope to gain your trust eventually."

All of that sounded like a bunch of sympathy. I had no desire to sit here and let someone coddle and feel sorry for me the whole time I was here. I was starting to feel all the sadness and pain I had been feeling turn into bitterness and pure anger. My emotions were now a mixture of wanting to cry and punch someone in the throat at the same time.

"Will you be willing to trust me, Kyrah?" she asked snapping me out of my thoughts.

"I guess..." I looked at Anthony and he smiled a little. I noticed he was still holding my hand.

"Great," she smiled, "Well, today is just a meet and greet to kind of figure out where your head is. We don't have to get too deep into anything if you don't want to. I just want to know a little about who Kyrah is, okay?"

I nodded, "O-okay."

We talked for a little bit, but she saw that I was nervous and not comfortable in any way, shape, or form, so we just closed the session. The whole time, I was sort of hoping Anthony would put his two cents in, but just like he said, he was only there for support. If he hadn't been holding my hand the whole time, I would've forgotten he was there.

"It was really nice meeting you, Kyrah. I do hope you come back so we can progress, and you can start trusting me. That's when the real process of progress begins. Here, let me give you my card so you can call whenever you need me, okay?" I nodded and took the card she gave to me. Anthony finally let go of my hand and looked at me.

"Can you go wait for me in the hallway for a sec? I'll be right out." I looked at him skeptically, simply because I didn't want to be alone in this foreign place. I hesitantly nodded and walked outside of her office and sat in one of the chairs in the hallway. I was going to zone out their conversation until I heard my name.

"Kyrah's been through a lot and a good chunk of it I put her through last year. I want her to trust me again. Seeing her like this is hard for me. What should I do? I mean, we're not dating anymore, but

I want to be there for her any way I can," Anthony asked desperately. *I hope he doesn't think he's the reason I'm like this...*

"Anthony, you can't blame yourself for this. She's just at a low point, but she will come out of this. You just have to keep praying for her. Give her some time. The emotions she's feeling right now are probably hard for her to communicate. But she'll open up. And believe me, she trusts you. If she didn't, she wouldn't be here right now."

It got quiet for a second, and I listened intently trying to figure out why they stopped talking. I thought about what Moriah said, and she was right. I already trusted Anthony. He had given me so many reasons to give him my trust in the past twenty-four hours.

"Don't worry, Anthony. She'll be fine. I feel in my spirit that she will."

"Thanks, Moriah. Tell Pastor Kendrick I said hello."

"Absolutely. See you soon." Anthony soon walked out of her office and stood in front of me.

"You ready?" I nodded and followed him out of the small, intimate church building. The ride back to school was silent. It wasn't a bad thing because it gave me time to think. And I was done talking for the day. I just wanted to go back to my room and lie in bed. School work was not even on my priority list, at the moment, which was not like me at all.

We arrived back at the school after a short ride. He walked me back to my room and I couldn't wait to get into my bed.

"Kyrah, wait." He stopped me from opening the main door to my suite by grabbing the hand that was so ready to open the door. I looked at him impatiently. "Did you like it? Would you go back?" I shrugged wanting this conversation to be over and done. A frustrated look grew on his face.

"Listen, I wanna help you. I really do. But I can't if you don't want it. Do you want me to help you, Kyrah?"

I looked down at my feet and sighed. "Anthony, I'm tired. I just want to go lie down." He shook his head and exhaled in frustration.

"A'ight. I'll talk to you later." He walked away, leaving me standing in the hallway alone. I opened the door and walked straight to my room. I closed my room door softly and locked it. A sudden urge to cry grew instantly because I knew Anthony was just trying to help. *But I don't need any help. I damn sure don't need counseling. I'm not depressed. I'll be fine...*

I sat on my bed and let the silent tears flow. There were so many thoughts running through my mind. And there were also multiple emotions going in and out of my body. I didn't know what to do. I knew Anthony was trying to help, but truth be told, I didn't really want it right now. On the other hand, I knew I needed help. Deep down inside, I knew this counseling was something I desperately needed. I just didn't want to admit it.

I looked at the clock on my desk that read 2:00. I turned my head towards the window and quickly became annoyed with how bright the sun was shining. Sighing, I got up, closed my blinds, and lay in my bed. I kicked off my shoes and hid under my blanket only to doze off into a much-craved slumber.

A knock on my bedroom door shook me out of my sleep, making me come back to my sad reality. I groaned as I hesitantly got out of bed to answer the door. I opened it slightly to find Tamra and Raynah standing there with hopeless smiles on their faces. On the inside, I smiled back at them, but apparently, I didn't because their faces became sad. I opened the door wider to let them in and I went to lie back in my bed. One of them had the audacity to turn the light on, but I didn't have the energy to say anything. They both sat down, Tamra at the foot of my bed and Raynah in my bean bag chair.

"How was the session?" Tamra asked. *"I don't wanna talk about it...* I stayed silent and hid more under my blanket, hoping she would stop asking me questions. "Kyrah?" I rolled my eyes.

"It was stupid. I'm not going back."

"What? Why not?" Raynah asked. Once again, I stayed silent. They both sighed. It was almost as if I could see them through my blanket; I knew disappointment was written all over their faces, and I couldn't bear to look at them.

"Well, we're gonna go and let you rest. You want some food? You need to eat," Tamra offered.

"I'm not really hungry."

"We'll get you some food anyway. Come on, Tam," Raynah said. I felt the presence of Tamra disappear from my bed and I heard the door close. The darkness was back, and I felt like I was finally able to relax again. Being around people these days made me anxious. I feared leaving my room because there was always a chance of running into Jesse. What if he was with another girl and acted like I was completely nonexistent? That's how he made me feel anyway. I felt tears coming and quickly fought them off. Crying would've made me even more exhausted than I already was. Instead, I closed my eyes, hoping to get a good night's sleep...

Chapter Six

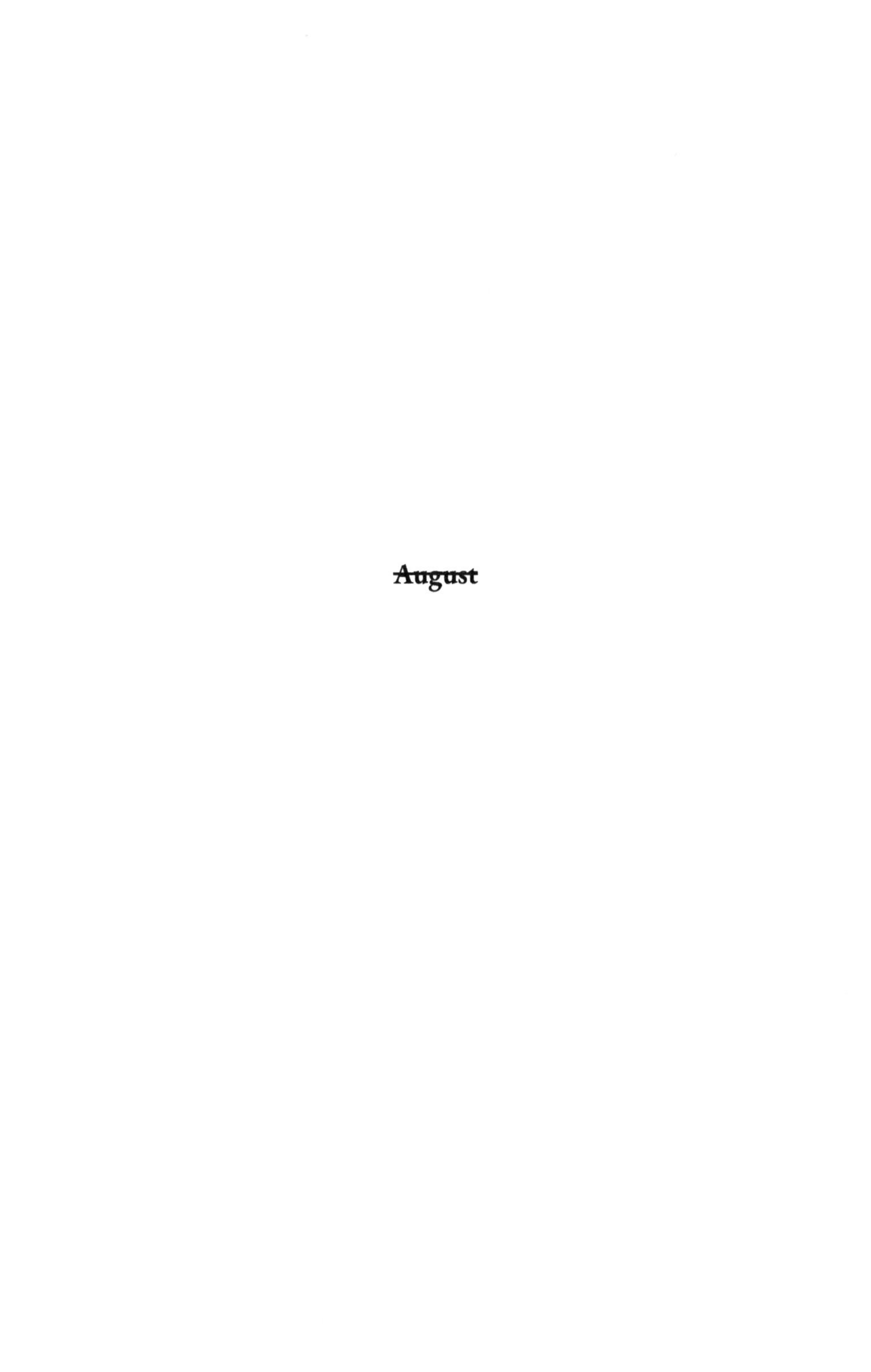

August

September.

October came fast. My mom has been calling me and I was convinced that someone told her I've been in this antisocial phase. I knew this behavior was getting out of hand because I didn't even feel like talking to her, even though I knew I needed to. I stared at my phone and looked at the five missed calls, all from her. I knew I wasn't going to return her calls, but I at least wanted to feel like I considered it. A sigh escaped my lips as I shut my phone off. My room was starting to look dull. Actually, everything was starting to look dull. But going outside of this room was not even on my list of desires. This dull room was the only place I wanted to be.

I lay down in the bed and stared at the ceiling. Going to my classes was the most activity my life consisted of at this point, but I started skipping classes this week. I didn't want to, but my body wouldn't allow me to do anything lately. Crying twenty-four-seven is draining, my body insisted that I stay in bed. So, I did. The crazy thing is I was starting to get used to this routine. *See? I told everybody I would be fine.*

Faint yelling from outside my door shook me out of my thoughts. The voices got closer making me nervous. I sat up quickly as the door swung open. *I thought I locked it...* A tall, familiar figure appeared from behind the door. My heartbeat quickened and instantly anger rose in my chest. Tamra appeared behind this monster; anger written all over her face.

"Kyrah, we need to talk," Jesse said as he walked inside my room. He tried to close the door, but Tamra was standing in the way.

"You're not closing this door and no, I will not leave. You're the reason she's like this!" He smacked his lips and looked at me.

"You not gon' tell her to leave?" I just stared at him, becoming angrier. The wound that I had been trying to ignore began to ache again. The pain came rushing back all at once. More tears flowed from my eyes as I stared at the person standing before me. Tamra saw my facial expression and faced Jesse.

"You need to leave," she said calmly. Jesse rolled his eyes and ignored her.

"Kyrah, baby, I need to talk to you."

"Don't call me that," I said with angry venom dripping from every word.

"Can we talk?"

"No. Get out." My voice was low, but the tone of it was very loud. He looked surprised by my response. He chuckled.

"Kyrah, for real. Stop playin'—"

"GET OUT!" Both he and Tamra looked at me surprised. He nodded and looked at her before walking out. My emotions were everywhere but where they needed to be. Anger was number one. I had never raised my voice like that before. But it felt good. Lashing out felt good.

"You okay?" Tamra asked. I looked at her forgetting she was there for a second since I was so deep in my thoughts. I nodded and looked down at my lap.

I had no clue what I was feeling right now. Suddenly another knock on the suite door caught both of our attention. Tamra went to answer it and I decided to lie back down. Zoning out from reality, I took in everything that had just happened. My heart began to ache as I pictured *his* face all over again. At one point, I would've done anything to see his face again so I could get some sort of explanation. Now, I didn't want to even think about him. A quiet sob fell from my lips, and I closed my eyes. Suddenly I felt a presence standing over me. I didn't dare open my eyes because I was afraid of who it was. The body kneeled to my eye level and softly touched my tear-stained cheek.

"Kyrah." I slowly opened my eyes to see Anthony. Every muscle in my body relaxed at the sight of his face. I hadn't realized it had been a while since I last saw him. He tried reaching out, but I would always ignore his calls or just one-word text him to let him know that I was okay. More tears came and I knew there was no stopping them, so I didn't try.

"Let me sit with you." I slowly sat up and made room for him to sit down at the foot of my bed.

"He was here..." I said wiping my face. He nodded and studied my face. I looked down at my hands which were now shaking from anger and sadness altogether. He reached over and held both of my small hands with his large hand. The urge to cry took over my body.

"Anthony, what's wrong with me?" I cried and cried and cried. He scooted closer and pulled me close to his chest for me to cry on.

"There's nothing wrong with you." I became annoyed by those words. He was telling me what he thought I wanted to hear. I pulled away from him and frowned.

"Stop doing that, Anthony! There is something wrong with me! I lost Jesse. I lost you... I don't know..." I could barely get my words out with my unstoppable tears. He took a deep breath as if he was choosing his words wisely.

"I... I really think you should call Moriah."

"Anthony, no."

"Kyrah—"

"Anthony, just drop it, okay? I'm not going back there. I'm not talking to someone who I don't know, and who's just gonna pity me. Alright? I don't need pity from anybody! From you either!" He frowned with a stunned expression.

"Kyrah, are you serious? You think I'm here because I pity you? I'm here because I care about you! Because I love you! You need help, and

I'm just trying to give you that! Why won't you just let me help you, Kyrah?" I can't say I was surprised he slightly raised his voice, but it caught me off guard. Tears formed in my eyes and didn't hesitate to fall down my face.

"Because I don't want to lose you again!" He stared at me as his mouth formed into a small "o". He tried to come closer to me, but I scooted away from him.

"It's easier for me to just push you away because I fear falling for you all over again and us ending up in the same place. I don't want to be in love anymore. I don't want to be with anyone anymore. The more you help me, the closer we get, the more it scares me. I just... Can't keep getting my heart broken, Anthony. I don't think I can handle it anymore." A soft sob came from my lips, and I looked away from him. He touched my leg which made me cry more.

"Kyrah, please... Call Moriah. I don't like seeing you like this. I know crying is good, but you've been crying constantly. I bet you don't even know why you're crying anymore, do you?" I sniffed and chuckled. I had to admit, he was right. I want to say all of this was Jesse's fault. Blaming him felt justified. But I knew that was a lie.

He smirked and continued, "Please, do it for yourself. Give yourself a break. I'm not pushing you to do anything, but you need to go back and talk to Moriah." I cringed on the inside because I knew he was right. It was about time I actually talked to someone and released these feelings. Crying just wasn't helping anymore and I think my body was starting to become immune to it.

I looked at Anthony and nodded. His face brightened a little and he smiled.

"I'll call her and tell her—"

"I think I should call her myself... And I think I'll go by myself this time."

"Are you sure?" An expression of concern covered his face. I nodded.

"Yeah. I need to go alone." He nodded and smiled.

Anthony gave me the address to the church, and I nervously pulled into a parking space. I was done making up excuses for not talking to someone. Here I was taking the first step to recovery. I took a deep breath before getting out of the car. I slowly walked into the church and was quickly greeted by the secretary.

"Hi! Kyrah?" she asked. I nodded and smiled timidly. "Okay, well you can go right back."

"Okay, thanks." Remembering the way to the office, I walked down the short hallway and knocked on Moriah's opened office door. She looked up from her computer and smiled.

"Kyrah, come on in," she greeted enthusiastically. The way I've been greeted since I've been here made me feel surprisingly welcomed. I sat in the same spot I sat in last time, and she sat in front of me.

"Okay, Kyrah," *here goes nothing...* "What made you decide to come back?"

I squirmed slightly, "I-I figured it was finally time to get out of this..." I drifted off unsure of how to finish the sentence. I know everyone saw me as depressed... Truthfully, so did I. But a part of me was still in denial. To my surprise, Moriah didn't respond. Instead, she waited patiently for me to finish. I looked at her desperately.

"I don't know what to call it...," I finally responded.

She nodded, "And that is completely understandable. May I ask why not?"

I swallowed and looked down at my lap. I played with the rips in my jeans.

"Because... I know I have symptoms of depression, but I just don't like to call it that... I don't like acknowledging it, I guess." I looked back at her, and she gave me a small smile.

"Okay, we won't call it that," she paused, "You know, sometimes we can appear to be depressed, but depression is sometimes really just a surface emotion. Underneath, we could be feeling withdrawn, inferior, empty, worthless... So, I would like to ask you... If you could give it a name, what would that be for you?"

I tried to blink away the tears that were forming in my eyes, but I was unsurprisingly unsuccessful. I shook my head.

"I think... I think I'm just hurt and confused. I feel like... I feel unworthy of love. Not even from just guys, but from God... When I first got to college, I was so focused on my relationship with Him and my schoolwork. I had never been in a relationship, never had sex, never drank. Then I met Anthony, and he changed everything. He introduced me to a whole new world. I was intrigued and so ready to be with him. I loved him. He loved me. So, I slept with him. Ever since that night, I never felt connected to God. I tried and tried to move past it, but I couldn't because sex became something I liked and felt guilty about at the same time. It's become harder for me to say 'no' to. And as of lately, talking to God is not even an option for me."

She looked at me with a warm expression like she was surprised I told her all that. To be honest, so was I. She nodded and smiled a little.

"You look relieved," she responded with a small smile. I let out a breath that felt like I had been holding for months.

"I honestly feel like I am... I'm sorry... I didn't mean to say all that. I just..." She cut me off, shaking her head with a slight frown.

"No, why are you apologizing? This is why you're here. This is what healing feels like. You're releasing. I don't want that to scare you. It's a good thing." I nodded and looked away.

"Kyrah, what I think I want to do is give you weekly assignments that I think will help you. This week, I want you to start praying again. Little simple prayers. Start talking to God again. I know He is just waiting to hear from you. And speak from your heart. If you're angry, tell Him. Sad? Tell Him. Need to cry? Do that. I just want you to start talking to Him. Do you think that's something you would be able to do?"

I thought about it for a few seconds. I hadn't talked to God, nor had I planned to in a long time. Not because I didn't want to, but because I genuinely felt like He didn't want to hear anything else I had to say. And I can't say I'd blame Him. Everything I've done in the past year... I wouldn't want to hear from me either. I slowly nodded, finally answering her question.

"Yeah... I can try." She smiled.

"That's all I'm asking for." We talked for another twenty minutes before we wrapped up the session. Part of me wanted to be skeptical about actually liking the session, but I could already feel a difference. I knew coming back was something I had to do, and I now realized that this was something I had to do for myself. Anthony couldn't do it for me, nor could Tamra, Raynah, or my mom. I had to recover and now is definitely the time.

"Will I be seeing you next week?" Moriah asked.

I smiled and nodded, "Absolutely." She smiled and gave me a hug.

"You call me anytime you need to talk. I'll see you next week, Kyrah."

"Thank you, a lot. See you next week." I walked out of the office, telling the secretary "Goodbye" on the way out of the church. I drove back to the school feeling like a few pounds of this weight I'd been carrying lifting.

Chapter Seven

Once I got to the dorms, I texted Anthony to let him know I was back. He quickly responded saying to meet him at his car. Slightly confused, I got out of my car and made my way to his. He met me there about five minutes later and greeted me with the biggest smile.

"Hey," he said giving me a hug.

"Hi." He opened the passenger door for me to get in then quickly hurried to the driver's side.

"Where are we going?" I asked skeptically. *Okay, I know I feel a little better, but I still wanna go lie down and sleep...*

"To dinner. I'm hungry and I figured we could catch up." I nodded and looked down at my lap. The ride to the restaurant was quiet, but it was pretty comfortable. We arrived in a short amount of time and were quickly seated. We sat in silence for a little while before Anthony broke it.

"So, how was it?"

I shrugged, "It was okay... I plan on going back." As comfortable as I was with him, I just didn't feel like I should talk to him about my session.

He smiled, "That's great, Kyrah. I'm really happy for you. Well, look... We don't have to talk about it. We can talk about something else." I nodded, silently thanking God for him saying that. A waitress soon came to our table to take our drink orders. After Anthony ordered an appetizer, she walked away, and he stared at me. Although I was looking down at the menu, I wasn't really reading it. It was more so me trying to avoid eye contact with this man.

"Kyrah, you okay?" I glanced at him and nodded, quickly looking back down at my menu. I didn't want things to be awkward between us, but they were. Having the first guy I've ever loved back in my life was something that I couldn't quite wrap my brain around and let myself be okay with.

"You know I know you, right? I can tell when something's bothering you. What's going on? Talk to me," he pressed. I hesitantly looked at him and sighed.

"I'm just thinking. That's all..."

"Okay, about what?" I looked at him and chose my words carefully. Fear of opening up to anybody, even if it's just a casual conversation, washed over me and I couldn't seem to find the words. He sighed and reached across the table for my hand. I hesitantly put my shaking hand in his. He rubbed his thumb across the back to calm me down. *He always could read me...*

"All I want to do is show you that I'm here. It won't be so easy to get rid of me this time. I will do whatever it takes to make you trust me again."

Tears threatened to fall from my eyes, and I looked away from his gaze. One tear made its way out of the corner of my left eye. I was feeling some sort of sorrow because I couldn't allow myself to fall for him again. I couldn't let him back in the way he desperately wanted to be.

"Anthony... I don't think I can do this with you again..."

"That's okay, Kyrah. But I want you to know that I love you and that I always will love you. I'm not here to try and get back with you. I just want you to know that you have me. No matter what. I'm not going anywhere, Kyrah."

More tears rolled down my face as I listened to him talk. I sat there trying to find the words to say.

"I-I-I... Anthony, you don't know what you're going to do..." He shook his head and stared deep into my soul.

"Mm-mm... I'm not leaving you. And I'm not lettin' you get away this time. I promise."

As much as I wanted to break eye contact, I just couldn't. I wish it was easy for me to let him back in. Every time he looked at me, it was like he could really see me. This new and improved Anthony was something I wasn't used to. This new Anthony made me forget about all the pain I was going through and all the past pain I had been through.

"Kyrah, I'm not asking you to take me back. You have every reason to be hesitant. I know how badly I hurt you. But I just want us to move forward, even if that's just as friends."

He stared into my eyes with deep sincerity. My heart began to ache as I looked back at him. I cleared my throat, carefully choosing my words before opening my mouth.

"I... would like for us to be close again. I'm just afraid of falling for you again," I finally responded.

"Don't worry about that. Let's just focus on right now. Focus on getting better. I'm just here to be the support system you need right now."

I carefully took in his gentle words and nodded.

"Okay." He grinned and nodded in response. The rest of dinner was quite pleasant, and I really enjoyed his company. I tried not to think of the possibility of me falling for him again. It was hard not to. I was in a very vulnerable state and the thought of being with someone who had already broken my heart made me anxious. I couldn't imagine going through another heartbreak. And as much as I could see the change in Anthony, I couldn't allow myself to trust him so soon.

Anthony drove us back to the school and he walked me to my room. He walked very closely to me giving me flashbacks to last year. We approached my door and stood in silence.

"Thanks for dinner. It was nice," I said looking at my feet.

He chuckled, "My pleasure. Can you look at me?" I hesitantly looked at him. He smiled warmly and stared into my eyes.

"Kyrah, you are beautiful. I hate seeing you like this. I really do. I know you don't fully trust me or trust me at all right now, but I really hope one day you can. I just want you to get better and focus on yourself right now. Let me be your support system. I'm here for you, you know that. I can only help you if you allow me to, though. But I'm just letting you know that you can't get rid of me easily. I'm not going anywhere. I promise you that." I smiled in response.

"Anyway," he continued, "thanks for having dinner with me. I enjoyed your company."

I looked at him not really knowing what to do or say. I just gave him a small smile and nodded.

"Thanks, Anthony. I appreciate it." He smiled and leaned in for a hug. He embraced me and I began to feel safe. I felt like he could protect me from the racing thoughts I felt coming once I stepped foot in my room. Tears began to form, and I couldn't fight them. He released his arms from around me. He wiped the tears from my eyes and kissed my forehead.

"See you tomorrow," he said while backing away. I nodded and walked inside my suite. Thankfully Tamra and Raynah weren't there so I was able to go straight into my room. I closed the door, locked it, and sat on my bed. *Enough socializing today. I'm ready to go to sleep...*

***

3 hours later...

I was lying in bed trying to get my thoughts to shut up. All I wanted to do was go to sleep, but my brain wasn't having it at all. I sighed and checked my phone to see what time it was. *Freakin' 10:00... Great.* Suddenly thoughts about reaching out to Anthony popped into my head. I didn't want to bother him with my issues. I'm sure he was tired of me by now. I thought about calling my mom, but I wanted to talk to her about all of this in person. Pastor Moriah was kind of out of the question because I figured it was too late. Anthony floated in my head once again and I eventually gave in. I needed to talk to somebody.

I rolled my eyes and sighed. I pulled up his name and texted him to see if he could come talk to me.

Anthony, are you busy? I waited literally one full minute before he texted me back.

Nah. What's up? You good?

Not exactly. Can we talk?

Of course. I'm on my way.

I slowly got out of bed and put some leggings on. I looked at myself in the mirror, hating the person staring back at me. She was unrecognizable. She had turned into someone who could no longer keep her emotions in check. I sighed and shook my head.

I heard the familiar knock on the suite door. As I was about to leave my room to open it, Tamra's door opened, and she beat me to it. I heard them talking while walking towards my room. The talking stopped and I heard Tam's door close before Anthony knocked on mine. I opened the door and saw him standing there with a concerned look on his face. I walked over to my bed and sat down with my back against the wall staring ahead. The only light source was from the night light near the door. He sat beside me and turned towards me.

"What's goin' on?" he finally asked.

I shrugged, "I've been trying to go to sleep for three hours, but my thoughts wouldn't shut up. I don't know why I texted you... I guess I just needed to talk, and you were the first person I thought of. I'm sorry..."

"Nah, it's cool. Don't apologize. I told you I'm here so let's talk. What's on your mind?"

I sighed. "Everything. I caught a glimpse of myself in the mirror and I don't recognize myself at all. I hate who I see when I look in the mirror."

"Why?"

"Because I no longer know *me*. I'm always sad and feeling down. It just feels like I'll always be here. I feel stuck. I wish I could just feel better." Tears formed as I talked. I rolled my eyes.

"And I'm so tired of crying", I finished sounding defeated. I finally looked at Anthony and he was listening to me. He took a deep breath before speaking.

"That's understandable. I have never gone through depression or anything near it before so I can't begin to imagine how you feel." I cringed inwardly at him saying I was depressed, but I couldn't even deny it anymore.

"But" he continued, "What you have to start doing is counteracting those thoughts you have about yourself. Start gettin' scripture in your brain and start speaking it to yourself. You'll start believin' it eventually."

I nodded. A small chuckle came from my mouth as I wiped the escaped tears.

"Who are you?" I asked chuckling.

He laughed, "I'm still me... Just new and improved, thank God." I smiled. I was starting to like the idea of talking and talking to Anthony was easy. He was a great listener and friend, which is exactly what I needed at this moment.

"Do you have a Bible sitting around somewhere?" he asked looking around. It was dark so I'm sure he couldn't really see anything.

"Yeah, there's one on my desk." He got up and walked to my desk. He turned the small lamp on beside my bed before sitting on my bed.

"Let's find a Bible verse now. Just to begin with. I have one in mind that kinda talks about what you're dealing with." I nodded waiting for him to continue. "Isaiah 30:15... 'For thus said the Lord God, the Holy One of Israel; In returning [to Me] and resting [in Me] you shall be saved; in quietness and in [trusting] confidence shall be your strength.'"

I looked at him puzzled.

"What does this mean?"

"God is basically sayin' that all you have to do is return to Him. He never left you. He's been waitin' for you to come back to Him all this time. Once you return to Him and truly seek after Him, you will be able to love yourself again. You'll be able to look at yourself in the mirror and speak life to yourself and your negative thoughts... All because you'll know how much God truly loves you."

More tears slipped from my eyes as I let his words sink into my heart. Everything he said began to calm my mind. I cried because I felt like I was having a conversation with God instead of Anthony. He grabbed my hands and guided me to the mirror. He stood behind me and looked at me through my reflection.

"You are fearfully and wonderfully made. God made you the way you are, and you are perfect. You can't hate what He created. He doesn't want you to feel like this. He doesn't want you crying all the time feeling sad. You're His child. He cares for you. Let Him take this pain away."

More and more tears came as I listened to Anthony and stared at myself. I turned around and faced him. He pulled me in for an embrace and let me cry on his chest.

"It's going to be okay, Kyrah... You won't be here forever."

Chapter Eight

I woke up the next morning to the sun shining in my eyes. Anthony and I talked for hours about everything. I even told him about what happened between me and Jesse and why he broke up with me. Anthony kept his composure even though I knew he was really bothered. We both ended up falling asleep around 3 in the morning. I fell asleep first and he made himself a little spot to sleep on the floor.

I looked on the floor to find Anthony still there knocked out. He was snoring quietly. I chuckled and lay back down. Suddenly I heard shuffling on the floor. Anthony groaned loudly as he stretched and sat up. He looked at me, slightly crossed.

"Hey," he said rubbing his eyes with his locs hanging loosely around his face.

"Hi... Do you have class today?"

"Nah. Today's my day off. I do have to work in a few hours, though." I nodded and looked at the ceiling. Admittedly I was sad that he was going to leave me only because I didn't want to be alone.

He showed me a completely different side of him that I legitimately enjoyed. I didn't want him to leave, even if it was just for a few hours.

He stood up and sat at the foot of my bed.

"Hey," he said insinuating for me to look at him. He placed his hand on my leg. I looked at him. He frowned. "We'll hang out once I'm off. I'll probably end up getting off early anyway. It's supposed to be a bad storm tonight, so my manager won't keep us there too long."

I nodded silently sighing in relief. I didn't want to start becoming dependent on Anthony being here for me 24/7, but he was all I had at the moment. He was my Godsend for the time being and I wanted to keep him around as much as possible.

"A'ight, I gotta go start getting ready. I'll see you later on. Go do something. Get out of this room." I nodded.

"O-okay..." The thought of leaving this room to go do something alone made my mind anxious. I tried not to let it show on my face. Anthony smiled as he stood up. He leaned down and planted a sweet kiss on my forehead. *Mission "don't fall for new and improved Anthony" is not working...* I watched him walk out of my room until he closed the door.

I must've laid in the same spot staring at the door for a whole thirty minutes. I wanted to get out of my room and go do something, but I couldn't bring myself to get out of bed. I guess I was still recovering from the day before from socializing so much. Turning my attention to the end dresser next to my bed, I saw my bible sitting there. I slowly sat up and grabbed it off the dresser. *What was that verse?* I sat there for a good two minutes trying to remember where the verse came from. A small groan of frustration fell from my lips. I decided to just open the Bible and see if I could remember by seeing the name of the book of the Bible.

As I opened the Bible, I saw that the bookmark was left right where the verse came from along with a note from Anthony. I frowned a little and read what he wrote:

> *Kyrah,*
>
> *I bookmarked this verse hoping that you would one day want to read it again. I had to squander around for a pen and some paper so I could write this while you were asleep. Hopefully, you remember everything I told you as you read over this verse again. Allow God to speak to you in so many different ways. Don't keep feeding into the negative thoughts. Let this be the beginning of your new way of thinking. I also pray that this is the beginning of us building a new relationship.*
>
> *I'll see you later. I'll be back as soon as I get off work.*
>
> *-Anthony*

I smiled a little and looked at the verse in the Bible that had been neatly highlighted. As I read, I remember everything that Anthony said the night before. A small tear escaped as every word he said replayed in my mind. I decided to pray as I sat there. This would be the first time in months that I talked to God. I was nervous to talk to Him in fear that He wouldn't hear me, but if it would help change my way of thinking, why not? I took a deep breath and got on the floor positioning myself to say a prayer on my knees. I closed my watery eyes and let the words flow from my heart:

"Dear God,

I know it's been a while since I've talked to You. I'm sorry for that. It's just been so hard not to feel guilty for everything I've done. I feel bad for even feeling depressed. I have tried to get through all of this on my own, but nothing is working. I didn't expect to still be dealing with this months after my breakup. I was angry at You, but then I missed

You after a while. The reason I didn't talk to You is because I felt like You didn't want to talk to me anymore. I still feel like that, but I figure I should at least try. Anyway... God, please help me. I don't want to feel like this anymore. And I don't know what else to do. If You are still listening to me, please help me... I need You..."

I opened my eyes and let out soft sobs. My face was soaked with tears. Admittedly, I felt like I could breathe for the first time in a while. I felt some peace of mind. A small smile grew on my face as I slowly stood up. My phone vibrated catching my attention. Anthony's name appeared on my screen saying he texted me.

Hey, you okay?

I quickly texted him back.

Yeah, I'm fine. I'm about to go to the park for a little while.

I put my phone down and went to find something to wear. I found some gray leggings and a large white T-shirt and decided to just keep it simple and comfortable. I quickly showered and got dressed. I washed my face and brushed my teeth before going back into my room to do something with my hair. My hair seemed to have a mind of its own, so I just left it in a big afro.

Tamra then came out of her room and walked into my room. She smiled at me like she hadn't seen me in years. I looked at her and smiled back as best as I could.

"Hey, where you off to?" she asked.

"I'm about to go to the park. I'm trying to get out of my room for a little while. Get some sunshine before the clouds come."

She nodded. "Can I come with you? I feel like we haven't hung out in forever."

I shrugged, "Sure. I could use some company." She smiled and went to her room to get dressed. As I waited for her, I decided to finally call my mom. I knew it would take Tamra a while to get dressed so I wasn't in a rush. She answered on the third ring.

"Hey, Kyrah."

"Hey, Mommy. How are you?"

"I'm alright, how are you? Are you okay?"

I sighed. I didn't exactly want to go into details about everything going on with me over the phone, so I just avoided the subject.

"Yeah, I'm okay... I'm actually planning to come home next week so we can talk."

"Well, what's going on?"

"A lot... But I'd rather talk about it in person. Just know I'm not pregnant."

She laughed in relief, and I laughed along with her.

"Okay, good to know. Now I'm not as worried. Well, alright. We'll talk about it next week." Tamra walked into my room fully dressed ready to go. I looked at her and signaled for her to give me a minute. She nodded and walked out of my room.

"Okay, mom. I'm about to go to the park with Tam. I'll talk to you later."

"Okay, homegirl. I'll talk to you later. Love you."

"Love you too." We said goodbye and I ended the call. I slipped on a jacket, and my Nike slides with some socks, grabbed my keys, and headed out of my room. Tamra followed me out of the suite, and we made our way downstairs to my car.

"It's so nice out right now. I hate that it's gonna storm," Tamra said as we waited in line for some ice cream. I nodded.

"Yeah, me too." The hot chocolate stand man then asked us how we wanted our hot chocolate. We told him our order and waited for him to make it. A few minutes later we paid and were handed our ice cream. We walked over to the swings and sat to talk. It was silent for a few minutes, but I didn't mind.

"So... What's going on with you and Anthony?" Tam asked out of the blue.

I shrugged, "Nothing. We're just friends." She chuckled.

"I never thought you guys would ever talk again, to be honest," she admitted. A small laugh came from my lips.

"Yeah, same here... He has really changed though. He's like a completely different person. Like, he prays, he talks about God so much... We completely swapped places from last year."

"Well, that's good, right? At least you don't have to worry about him being a jerk anymore." I nodded.

"Yeah, I guess so..."

We stayed at the park for almost two hours just talking. She did most of the talking and I was mainly thinking. As soon as we both noticed the rain clouds, we decided it was time to go back to school. We arrived back at the school after a short ride just in time for Tamra to meet her study group. She thanked me for letting her tag along and we parted ways.

I sat on my bed and stared at the wall in front of me. Truthfully, I was pretty tired from being out of my room, but I was proud of myself for at least trying. Interrupting my thoughts, my phone began ringing slightly startling me. Anthony's name appeared on my screen. I quickly answered.

"Hello?"

"Hey, Kyrah. I'm off earlier than I thought so I'll be back soon. You hungry?"

"Uh, not really... but I haven't eaten today so I guess I should eat something."

He chuckled, "Yeah, you should. You want some Zaxby's?" I smiled at the fact that he remembered my love for their food.

"Yeah, that's fine."

"Okay, I know what you want so I'll let you know when I get back to the school."

"Okay." We said our goodbyes and hung up. I guess it was perfect that he called about food because my stomach growled as soon as we got off the phone. Minutes passed but it felt like I had been waiting for hours because I kept checking the time. I thought about watching TV to help the time pass by faster but nothing on TV interested me at this point. I scanned over my room to find something to occupy myself with. My eyes landed on the book I was reading the day Anthony and I reconnected.

I got up and grabbed my bookmarked book off the desk. Once I returned to my bed, I comfortably wrapped myself in my warm blanket and began reading. Instantly I became lost in the storyline of the book and lost track of time. My stomach growled a few times, but I didn't pay it any attention since I was so wrapped up in the story. Suddenly, someone was knocking on my door. I looked up from the book puzzled because I thought Anthony was going to let me know when he got here. My heartbeat quickened in fear that it was the last person I wanted to see. Jesse. Scenarios of how seeing him after finally beginning to heal could go wrong. The door slowly opened and revealed Anthony with arms full of food. I sighed in relief when I saw his face.

"Hey, I texted you," he said with a slight grin. I frowned and looked at my phone. His name was on my screen revealing that he had indeed texted me twice. I chuckled.

"Sorry. I was reading and wasn't paying attention." He set the food and drinks on my desk and deciphered what belonged to who.

"It's okay. I know how you get when you're into a book." He smirked and handed me my food and drink. I smiled and looked at my box of delicious food.

"You remembered," I said with a warm heart.

"Of course. I could never forget." He sat at my desk with his food. He blessed both our food, and we dug in. We discussed our days and what we did. He told me in detail what he did at work and how he was happy his boss let him off early. I told him how I went to the park with Tam for a little while. He smiled as I told him about my little adventure.

"I'm glad you got out of the room. I'm proud of you."

I shrugged, "Yeah, it wasn't too bad. I had to mentally prepare myself to be around people though."

He chuckled and nodded, "Understandable."

We sat and ate while holding small talk for a while. Halfway into our meal the storm started. It wasn't so bad at first, but it eventually got louder and louder. I stopped eating and stared out my window as the rain poured. Something about the rain was unusually calming and mesmerizing. I snapped myself out of the hold of the rain and looked down at my food. I took a small bite of a French fry and looked up to find Anthony looking at me.

"What?" I asked clueless.

"You okay? You kinda zoned out." I nodded and shrugged.

"The rain is peaceful... I normally hate it when it rains and normally storms kind of scare me... But it's calming right now. I'm not sure why." I glanced out of the window again but quickly looked back at Anthony.

"I love the rain," he began. "I always have. It always puts me to sleep, even when I was little. My mom actually used to pray for rain sometimes so I would sleep without giving her grief about it." I chuckled at the thought of Anthony being overly rambunctious enough for his mom to have to pray for rain.

"But even now," he continued, "when I have a hectic day or I just can't sleep or rest or whatever, I pray for rain myself to help me sleep."

I stared at him listening closely. I closed my plate of food and set it aside. Crossing my legs, I grabbed a blanket and wrapped it around me, making myself comfortable in anticipation of more childhood stories from Anthony. He chuckled frowning slightly.

"What you doin'?" he asked.

I giggled, "I wanna hear more stories about your childhood. It'll help take my mind off me for a while." I suddenly realized that although we dated for a short while last year, we never really knew each other. At the moment, I was pretty intrigued to learn more about him. He smiled a little and nodded.

"A'ight. Well, make some room so I can sit with you." I instantly scooted towards the head of my bed to make room for him. He closed his empty plate and made his way to my bed. He sat beside me and faced me. I looked at him waiting for him to start.

"Go ahead," I said a little eagerly.

He laughed, "Wait, I gotta think of a good one." I rolled my eyes playfully. He finally thought of one and began telling it.

***

Hours passed and we were still talking and laughing. We alternated between each other's childhoods, and both told crazy stories. It was a good conversation that I needed, and it helped me keep my mind off my issues. The rain hadn't let up at all, so we still had the sound of a storm and raindrops in the background.

"I've learned a lot about you that I would have never known... I actually didn't expect you to go through a punk-rock phase", Anthony said while laughing hysterically. I laughed along with him.

"Don't judge me, please. I was trying to find who I was at the time. I'm so embarrassed to even think about that." He laughed harder and shook his head.

"Wow... Well, I'm sure you were just as cool then as you are now." I shrugged and looked down.

"I like to think that I've figured out who I am by now, but I'm starting to think that I'm not even close."

He chuckled, "Well, I don't think there's anything wrong with that. You have the rest of your life to figure out who you are and what you wanna be and all'at. Why do you always put a time limit on yourself?" I looked at him and carefully thought about my answer. Honestly, I didn't really have one because I had never really thought about it that way.

"I'm not sure, actually... I guess I just feel like I have to have everything figured out. You know, I don't want to let anybody down or disappoint myself for that matter." I looked away and then looked back at my lap. He sighed and paused for a second.

"Hey... You're not disappointing anybody. Stop bein' so hard on yourself, baby girl. You're doin' the best you can. Just take it one day at a time. I honestly believe that one day you'll grow into who you're supposed to be, and you won't even realize it when it happens."

I smiled and nodded. Taking in every word he said, I tried to think of something else to talk about.

"Sooo... Got any more stories?" I asked.

He chuckled and thought about it for a second. He finally thought of another one and we told stories for pretty much the rest of the night. *This may be something I could get used to...*

Chapter Nine

I t was now the following weekend, and I was planning on going home to talk to my parents to let them know what's been going on with me. Truthfully, I was nervous, and I secretly wished I could bring Anthony with me.

He sat in my room with me as I packed for the weekend trip home. My mind was all over the place and as a result, I was literally just throwing random clothes in my bag. Anthony chuckled and I looked at him puzzled.

"What?" I asked clueless.

"Um, don't you wanna pay attention to what you're packin'?" he responded still laughing a little. I looked down at my bag. I sighed and closed my eyes in frustration.

"Hey, what's wrong?" he asked interrupting my almost anxiety attack. I shook my head.

"I'm so nervous to tell my parents about what's going on with me. I don't know why... What if they don't understand me or they're ashamed of me? Or worse, they don't care?" I sat beside Anthony and tried my best to swallow the tears that threatened to escape my eyes. He placed his hand on my thigh and placed his other hand under my chin making me look at him.

"Don't worry about that. Everything'll be fine. Your parents love you. I'm sure they'll just wanna know how they can help. Just breathe." I bit my bottom lip slightly and nodded as I looked into his eyes. We stayed like that for a while until he cleared his throat and looked down. He removed his hand from my thigh and continued to look down at his lap.

"So, you have everything you need? I'll help you take your stuff to your car," he said breaking the obvious tension between us. *Not everything... I need you...*

I nodded, "I think so... Either way, I'll be back Sunday, so it doesn't really matter." He smirked and nodded.

"Well, let's get you settled."

We both got up and he grabbed both of my bags. I grabbed my keys and phone, and we walked out of the room. I said goodbye to Tamra and Raynah, and we headed out of the suite and downstairs to the parking lot. He placed my bags in the back seat of my car and opened the driver's side door for me. He stood in front of me and gave me a reassuring look.

"I wish I could go with you [*So do I...*], but I have a feeling you won't need me. You'll be fine. Call me, though. I'm here if you wanna cry over the phone or just need to feel like I'm there with you. Be safe and lemme know when you get there." I nodded and smiled weakly. He gave me a long hug. I didn't want him to let go. I felt so incredibly safe in his arms. We removed our embrace from one another, and I hesitantly got in the car. He leaned down and kissed my cheek before closing the door. He was honestly just making it harder for me to be without him for a few days... But maybe this is what I needed. I was afraid that I was becoming too attached to him and too dependent on his presence.

I waved at him one last time and drove off. I looked in the rearview mirror and watched as his figure disappeared into the distance. The drive home was not that long since my mind was running so much. I practiced how this conversation with my parents would go over and over about a hundred times. I prayed, but my nerves wouldn't calm down and my hands wouldn't stop sweating.

By the time I pulled up to my house, I was completely out of energy from all that thinking. I got all my things from the backseat, locked my car, and headed inside the house. My parents were out on a date, and I figured they would be back late, so I decided to just put the conversation off until the next day. I went into my room and looked around. I miss being at home more than anything. I put all my things in a corner and sat on my bed. My sister moved out over the summer, so I officially had the room to myself.

I made myself comfortable on my bed and pulled out my phone. *Oh yeah, I need to text Anthony...* I quickly pulled up his name and texted him.

> Hey, I made it home.

He responded within a minute like he had been waiting for me to text him.

> Good... Glad you made it safely. I'm still at work, but I'm on break.

I kicked my shoes off and lounged in bed as I texted him back. We texted back and forth for a little while until he had to get back to work. I didn't really expect us to talk much this weekend due to him working overtime and getting off super late, but I figured it would probably be a good thing. I glanced at the clock on my dresser which read 10:00 p.m. My eyelids grew heavier by the minute, and I soon realized that I could not wait for my parents to come back. I decided to change into my pajamas and get ready for bed. The only source of light came from my nightlight in the far corner which was perfect enough to help me doze off into a deep sleep...

***

Ring Ring!* I groaned in aggravation as my phone rang loudly at twelve o'clock in the morning. I silently cursed at myself for forgetting to put my phone on *Do Not Disturb*. My phone continued to ring, and my screen lit up with Anthony's name. Wild butterflies were awakened just by seeing his name and I couldn't control them. I answered the phone completely forgetting that my sleepy voice would be in full effect.

"Hello?" I answered sleepily.

"Hey, were you asleep?" I yawned silently.

"Yeah, but it's fine. Are you okay?"

"Yeah, I'm fine. I just wanted to hear your voice... I've gotten used to bein' with you every day." He chuckled. I smiled to myself.

"Well, I'm glad you called. I wish you could be here with me for this conversation with my parents tomorrow." He sighed.

"Yeah, I know... You know I would be right there holding your hand if I ain't have to work overtime all weekend."

"I know..."

"Don't worry, baby girl. You'll be fine, a'ight?" I nodded as if he could see me.

"Okay."

We talked for about an hour, but I mostly listened as he told me about his long shift at work. I didn't mind listening to him; his voice was so deep and soothing. It helped distract me from my own thoughts. Every time he spoke, I couldn't help but give him my undivided attention and listen closely to every word that fell from his lips.

"So will it be okay if I call you again tomorrow night when I get off work?" he asked slyly.

I chuckled, "I don't know. I have to check my schedule. I think I have sleep penciled in for tomorrow night, but I'll see what I can do." He laughed a hearty laugh.

"Wow. Well, how did I manage to get penciled in tonight?"

"You didn't. You just got lucky because I wanted to talk to you." He continued laughing and I joined him. Moments later he finally calmed down enough to talk.

"You are somethin' else. I guess I'll let you finish your appointment with sleep, then. I could catch a few Z's myself."

I suddenly became a little sad. This is where my separation anxiety started to settle in: whenever we had to say goodbye. I didn't want to get off the phone with him because it felt like he was here with me, but I knew we couldn't stay on the phone forever.

"Oh... okay," I said disappointed. He chuckled.

"I can hear how tired you are in your voice. Don't worry, I'll call you tomorrow night. Just make sure you put me in your schedule, a'ight?" I laughed lightly.

"Yes sir. Thanks for calling me. Goodnight, Anthony."

"No problem, baby girl. Goodnight, Kyrah." I hit "end" on my phone and placed it beside me. I stared at the ceiling trying to make myself go back to sleep. After looking at nothing for thirty minutes, I finally dozed off...

I woke up the next morning wishing I was still asleep, but I knew I had to face the music of the day. It was time to talk to my parents and explain what I'd been dealing with. One thing, in particular, I knew I wasn't sure about was telling them about how my breakup with Jesse went down. My mom knew about me losing my virginity to Anthony last year, but everything after that she had no clue about. My dad, on the other hand, knows absolutely nothing. He's completely oblivious to the mistakes I've made, and I was honestly starting to think it was best that way.

After concluding that I would just tell them that I've been experiencing some form of depression and that I've been talking to a counselor at a "friend's" church, I finally got out of bed. I quickly showered and took care of every other part of my hygiene routine, and lastly got dressed. Staring in the mirror, my brain began to tempt me to just let it go and deal with this on my own. *Would it really hurt if they didn't know? Is that so bad? I've been dealing with this alone for all this time, so it wouldn't be detrimental to keep figuring it out by myself.* I shook those thoughts out of my head and walked out of my room to meet my parents downstairs. When I got down there, they were sitting in front of the TV. I took a deep breath and sat on the couch on the opposite side of the room.

"Can we talk?" I asked lowly. They both nodded and my dad turned off the TV.

"What's going on?" he asked. I hesitantly looked at them, trying to find the words to say. Too many thoughts were swimming through my mind, and I silently prayed for God to help me.

I took another deep breath and let it all out. I told them about my random breakup with Jesse and how I stopped going to classes because I couldn't get myself out of bed. I expressed how down I've been and that I've been feeling out of touch with God and myself. They both looked at me with sad expressions. I couldn't quite read them and figure out what they might've been thinking, but at this point, I didn't care. All I cared about was just putting everything out there on the table.

"So, I've been seeing someone at a friend's church for like counseling. I'm not sure if it's helping yet, but I'm willing to give it some more time," I finished. I exhaled in relief. Honestly, I was very proud of myself for going through with this and telling them everything... Well, mostly everything.

"Do you need to come home? I don't want you stuck in your room all day. Why didn't you talk to us sooner? We could've helped," my mom said with a cracked voice. I shrugged as tears spilled from my eyes.

"I didn't want to disappoint you guys." They both joined me on the couch I was sitting on, Mom on my left and Dad on my right.

"We care about you, and we don't want you to feel like you can't come talk to us. Out of all your siblings, you are the most soft-spoken, and we know how you like to try to figure things out on your own. But some things you can't figure out alone. We want to be here for you through this and we will help in any way we can. If you feel like you need to come home, then we will take care of that. If you feel like you can finish the year off, then we support that, too. But don't feel like you have to go tough this out alone. Depend on the people that God placed in your life. We love and care about you very much."

By the time my dad finished talking, my face was soaked with tears. All I could do was nod and hug them. Admittedly, I felt lighter after releasing that large weight that sat on my back 24/7.

"I love you guys," I said.

We decided to go get some brunch as a family after calling up the rest of my siblings. My oldest brother and sister were at their own places when we called them, and my youngest brother was hanging out with some of his college friends in his dorm. He went to school in our hometown but stayed on the campus to still experience being on his own. We all met at a restaurant and enjoyed being in one another's company. It felt good to be around my whole family and just joke around. *This is just what I needed...*

That evening, Anthony called me as he had promised. We talked for a long time, and I told him how everything went. He was so happy for me and assured me that I would always have him in my corner. I have to admit that he has truly been my backbone throughout all of this. I would have never thought we would ever be this close after everything that went down between us last year. But I'm glad that he is back in my life.

After talking to him for a few hours, we decided to call it a night since it was late, and he had to work one more overtime shift. That night I was able to sleep better than I had in a while. I could easily blame it on the fact that I had been on the phone so late, but I genuinely believe that it was because I had finally started the real healing process...

Chapter Ten

Anthony and I were chilling in one of the study rooms in the library. I agreed to go with him because I figured it would be nice to get out of my room for a bit. While he was typing away on his computer, I went to look for a book to read.

I ended up in the fiction-romance section, of course.

Hmm... What to read... I thought to myself.

My eyes roamed the shelves until they landed on Perfect Chemistry by Simone Elkeles. I checked out the book and headed back to the study room. I sat across from Anthony and made myself comfortable by resting my feet in another seat in front of me.

I began reading the book and immediately got sucked into it. I am admittedly an absolute sucker for romance novels... well, novels in general. As I read, I could feel my facial expressions changing as I carefully took in each word. Minutes into reading, I felt Anthony staring at me.

"That book better be good, Kyrah," he joked. I rolled my eyes and laughed.

"It is, thank you very much. I'm almost on the second chapter." He chuckled.

"You kidding? You literally just sat down and started reading." I blushed and shrugged.

"I'm a fast reader", I responded. He smiled.

"What do you like about reading? I wish I was into books like you. You make it look fun." I smiled a little, eager to answer.

"Well... It gives me a chance to live in a different world for a little while. I put myself in the narrator's shoes and get to experience a different life. It may not be real, but it feels real. I have a habit of getting too caught up sometimes, though." I laughed a little and he laughed too.

"That's interesting... So basically, you a nerd." I smacked my lips and laughed.

"Whatever. I'm the coolest nerd you'll ever meet." He smirked and stared at me. I blushed as my face began to burn with shyness.

"What?" I asked as I looked down at the book to avoid his gaze. He shook himself out of his thoughts and chuckled nervously.

"Oh-uh nothin'... Nothin'. My bad. I was just thinking about something. I ain't mean to stare."

I nodded and silently began to read again. I did want to know what he was thinking about. Suddenly curiosity overloaded my brain. I mean, obviously, if he was staring so deeply into my soul it was something I should want to know. I cleared my throat before speaking.

"Soooo... What were you thinking about?" I asked breaking the silence that had taken over the room. I kept looking down at my book and acted like I was still reading. He looked at me and frowned a little.

"Nothin' important. Don't worry about it." I rolled my eyes and looked at him.

"Anthony, you have literally been picking my brain since we started hanging out again. It's only fair I pick yours now. Besides, you know I'm nosey." He chuckled and surrendered.

"A'ight, fine. I was, uh, just thinkin'... How much I've been enjoying getting to know you more. I really missed you, Kyrah. Like, you have no idea." I smiled, looking at his face. I searched his eyes to see if he had more to say. He sighed and returned my gaze. He slowly got up and came to my side of the table. I took my feet out of the chair so he could sit down. He carefully and gently removed the book from my hands and held them in his warm, large hands. He searched my eyes and smirked.

"You remember when I told you that I felt like God brought you into my life for a reason?" I nodded still captured in his gaze. He spoke very lowly in his already deep voice.

"I still believe that" he continued, "and now I know that's true. I also know that right now we're friends and I can't help but think that this is how we should've done things last time. But I'm just glad I have another chance with you. Right now, we're not ready to be together, but I want you to know that I'm going to pursue you. You deserve that and more. I hate that it took me this long to see that and I'm sorry. Just know that I feel in my spirit that you are the one for me.

"I can feel a nudge in my spirit every time I see you. It may not be time right now because I want to just be here to make sure you're taking care of yourself... But know that when God gives me the okay one of these days, I'm going to make this happen. And this time, I'm going to love and cherish and pursue you like I should've done last time. I love you, Kyrah. I always will."

I sat there speechless. I wanted to hug him, but my hands felt too safe in his. I scooted my chair closer to him and hugged him tightly. I let out a sigh of relief. I had been having these feelings and thoughts about

Anthony and I being together, but I never thought it could happen again. I removed myself from the hug and looked into his beautiful brown eyes.

"I love you, too, Anthony. I always will." He smiled widely and pushed some strands of my wild afro behind my left ear. I watched closely as his gaze moved from my eyes to my lips. He bit his bottom lip slightly, then looked down in defeat.

"I wanna kiss you… So badly… But that would make things more complicated." I nodded and looked down. He put his hand under my chin and made me look at him.

"But I promise the next time our lips touch, we'll both know it's the right time." I smiled and nodded.

Shortly after, we decided to head back to the dorms. We walked silently, but closely back to our suites. He walked me to the door of my suite. He looked at me waiting for me to say something. His locs hung loosely on both sides of his face. I admired him before speaking.

"I really appreciate you telling me, y'know, all of that. I was really hoping you felt that way. I'm looking forward to our first date in the future." He smiled as he pulled me in for our last hug of the night.

"I am too. I'll see you tomorrow, a'ight? Get some rest." I nodded.

"Okay. Goodnight, Anthony."

"Goodnight, Kyrah." We let go of one another and I hesitantly unlocked my suite door. I looked up at him once more and walked into my suite. He smiled and nodded his head towards me before walking away.

I walked to my room in a daze. It was almost like we didn't want to leave each other. We've been spending so much time together, but tonight was different. I quickly changed into my pajamas and turned off every light except my night light. I lay in bed and stared at what I could make of the ceiling, engulfed in my thoughts.

I wonder if he's thinking about everything now, too. What does this mean, God? I always knew something was special about Anthony… I just accepted that we would probably be stuck as friends… Am I ready to be with him again, though? He's such a different person now. Am I good enough for him? What does he see in me?

I could slowly feel myself walking into an anxiety attack. I closed my eyes and took a few deep breaths. My phone vibrated interrupting my obsessive thoughts. Thankfully. I checked my phone and saw that Anthony texted me.

> Forgot to let you know I'm in my room, lol. I'll see you tomorrow, babygirl. Sleep peacefully.

I smiled and quickly responded.

> Lol, thanks for letting me know. See you tomorrow, love.

I slowly drifted off to sleep after I pressed send.

***

I woke up the next day in a daze. Everything from last night replayed in my mind and I couldn't stop the wild butterflies in my stomach. I wanted so badly for Anthony to kiss me, but he was right. It would only complicate things. I was finally getting over everything that happened with Jesse and I didn't want to set myself up for another heartbreak. I needed to give myself a break. Two relationships in one year? That's definitely pushing it.

I slowly sat up and looked around my room. I stood up and opened my room door to go to the bathroom when there was a loud knock on the main door. Thoughts of ignoring it and acting like it didn't even happen swam through my mind, but I figured it might've been important. I sighed and walked towards the door since nobody else was going to answer it. Without looking in the peephole, I slowly opened the door. *Oh no...*

"Jesse, w-what are you d-doing here?" I asked nervously. I was trying to hold all my anxiety in and not have a meltdown in front of him. I didn't want to give him that power anymore. He sighed.

"Listen, we gotta talk at some point. You need to stop avoidin' me." He looked at me with begging eyes. I tried to look away, but I couldn't. Part of me wanted to admit that he was right, but the majority of me knew that it would be a bad idea to let him see the vulnerable side of me.

"Jesse... I don't think talking to you would make a difference. I j-just don't—"

"You don't have to right now, but let's just meet up and go to the caf or somethin' later. We can talk then... Just us." I thought about it. I couldn't keep running from Jesse.

"Fine. We can meet at the caf at 12." He smiled in relief and nodded.

"A'ight, bet. I'll see you then. Thanks, Kyrah." I hesitantly nodded and closed the door as he walked away.

I was honestly dreading this meet-up with Jesse, but I knew there was no avoiding it, or him, anymore. As I walked to the cafeteria, I silently prayed and asked the Holy Spirit to control my tongue and my emotions so that I wouldn't act out of character. After all, I was meeting up with the man who broke my heart and left me wondering where we went wrong.

As I entered the cafeteria, I instantly regretted it as soon I spotted him sitting in a booth with a girl. I rolled my eyes and slowly walked over there. He looked up and saw me coming and quickly dismissed the girl who was sitting so close to him.

"Hey," he greeted with a smile.

"Hi," was all I said.

"Sooo... Thanks for coming. I didn't think you would—"

"Jesse, can we please just cut the small talk? What is it you want to talk about?" His eyes grew big, but he relaxed after he realized I wasn't in the mood for his charm. He sighed deeply and rubbed his hands over his face as if he was trying to think of what to say.

"A'ight... First, I just want to apologize for hurtin' you. You didn't deserve that, especially not how I ghosted you after." He looked at me and waited for me to respond. I just nodded and looked down.

"Second," he continued, "I have to admit something to you that may cause you to not want to talk to me ever again, but I'm askin' you to at least hear me out, a'ight?" My heart began to beat fast because deep down, I knew what he was about to say. The one thing that I tried so hard not to assume, but I knew it was coming. I looked at him with glossy eyes and waited for him to say it. He took a deep breath before speaking.

"I cheated on you while we were together... More than once. [*Oh...*] Kyrah, look, I'm so sorry. I didn't mean to, it was just every time we got close to havin' sex, you would stop it and it would frustrate me and I couldn't help—"

"Jesse," I said my voice cracking, "please, save your excuses because I don't really care why you did it." Tears spilled from my eyes as I talked. "I honestly think it would've been better if I had never known that, but since you told me, it was just confirmation of what I had hoped wasn't true... But you were right about two things: you are sorry, and I don't want to speak to you ever again. We don't have to continue this conversation; I've heard all I needed to hear. I'll leave you to your girlfriend. Goodbye, Jesse." I quickly got up and walked away, completely ignoring him calling after me.

I felt as if I couldn't get to my room fast enough. Tears drenched my face completely and pain settled in my heart, but I also felt a sense of relief. *I thought this was over... I thought I was done with feeling like this... I should have never gone to talk to him... I needed closure... But I think I would've been better off not knowing anything.* I slowly sat on my bed and sobbed. My chest was aching from the pain I felt. Jesse had turned into the monster of my nightmares. I could no longer look at him the same. It was as if everything he said to me last year was just to make him feel better about only wanting to be with me physically. I couldn't stop crying, but I knew I couldn't let him have this power over me anymore. I walked over to my mirror and thought about the night Anthony spent with me and how he reminded me that I had to counteract my negative thoughts. I wiped my tears and stared at the girl in the mirror.

I'm never good enough. "Yes, I am. I'm more than enough."

I'm only good for sex. "I am fearfully and wonderfully made. I am worth more than rubies."

God will never forgive me. He is punishing me. "He forgives me, and He is my strength."

No one will ever love me. "Jesus loves me."

Chapter Eleven

I spent a couple of days thinking about everything that happened. I tried talking to God more and encouraging myself. I even went to another counseling session with Moriah, which is getting easier for me. Opening up has been difficult for me, but I really appreciate how she made the atmosphere comfortable enough for me to be a little more vulnerable each session.

It's now Sunday and Anthony reached out to me to see if I wanted to go to church with him. At first, I wasn't really feeling it, but I figured it would probably help keep my mind off of this week's events. He told me to dress casually because his church was very "chill", so I didn't put much effort into my outfit. I just picked out a gray boyfriend T-shirt and some blue jeans with holes in the knees. I paired it with some black Ugg boots and a long cardigan. Like always, I didn't really know what else to do with my hair, so I styled it in my signature puff. Once I finished dressing and doing my hair, I stared into the mirror.

"Makeup or no makeup?" I thought long and hard about it. I sighed and shook my head "No".

"Nah", I said as I walked away from the mirror. I put on my glasses and waited for Anthony to come to my room. Suddenly, there was a knock on the door. I grabbed my phone, my purse, and my Bible and went to greet him at the door.

A sigh of relief escaped my lips when my eyes landed on Anthony's face. He smiled and gently pulled me in for a hug. I inhaled his cologne and exhaled into his embrace. We let go of one another with smiles on both our faces.

"You ready?" he asked. I nodded and he motioned for me to walk before him.

We walked very closely to one another on the way to the car while holding small talk. Once we got in the car, he turned on some Christian rap music and began bobbing his head. To this day, I'm still shocked at the man before me. He was a completely different person. At first, there was something about this whole change that I didn't think was really genuine, but now, I can definitely see that he has really changed. I smiled to myself while thinking about him. He glanced at me, making me blush. He smirked.

"I missed you this week, beautiful. I'm not used to not seeing you every day," he said.

I nodded, "I was thinking the same thing. But I think I really needed this week. I made an effort to go to my classes. I left all of them early, but I tried." I shrugged and he chuckled.

"Hey, you're right. You tried. That's all that matters." I giggled a little.

"Anything else happen this week?" he asked. I silently debated in my head if I wanted to tell him about my meeting with Jesse. Knowing that it wasn't the best timing, I opted to wait.

"Yeah, but we can talk about it later." He nodded.

"Bet. No problem. We can go get some lunch after church if you want." I smiled.

"I'd like that."

Church was good. It was actually better than I expected it to be. It was a good distraction, which I definitely needed. I was finally able to meet the pastor, who Anthony spoke so highly about. He was a pretty nice guy. As expected, he was rather young-looking like Moriah.

The ride to the restaurant Anthony and I decided on was nerve-racking. This was only because I was nervous to tell him about Jesse. I wasn't sure how he would react and if he would be really bothered by it.

Does it really matter, though? He's not my boyfriend...

We arrived shortly and were seated as soon as we walked in. We both looked over our menus as we waited for our waiter. Shortly, a young guy about our age walked over to us to take our drink orders.

"What can I get you two to drink?" he asked with a bright smile.

"I'll have a sweet tea," Anthony said. The waiter nodded and looked at me.

"Water, please?" He nodded with a warm smile and walked away. It was quiet for a little bit as we continued to look over our menus. Me being me, I was absent-mindedly looking at the food options before me.

"I know you're not even reading the menu," Anthony said chuckling. I took a deep breath and placed the menu down. I gave a small laugh.

"You're right."

The waiter came back with our drinks and took our food orders. I had no idea what to get so I just settled for the appetizer sampler. The waiter took our menus and left us alone.

"You wanna talk about it?" he asked looking me in my eyes. I shrugged.

"I would end up telling you, anyway." He smirked and nodded. I took a deep breath and prepared myself to tell the story. I gathered my thoughts before speaking.

"Okay, first you have to promise not to get mad," I started. He frowned a little but relaxed when I eyed him. He nodded and sighed.

"Okay...," I continued, "the day after we hung out at the library, Jesse stopped by... He asked to meet up. I figured I couldn't avoid him forever, so I agreed. He apologized for hurting me but then proceeded to tell me that he had cheated on me multiple times in our relationship. I don't know why... but I felt like my heart was broken all over again." My voice became shaky. I didn't want to cry over Jesse anymore so I swallowed my tears the best I could. I searched Anthony's facial expression and was shocked to see how calm he was.

I cleared my throat, "Are you upset?" He frowned a little and shook his head "No".

"Nah, of course not. Why would I be upset?" he asked genuinely. I shrugged.

"I don't know. I thought maybe you would be mad about him cheating on me..." He glanced down before looking back at me. He sighed.

"Babygirl, I don't care about him. I only care if you're okay or not... Are you okay?"

"I wasn't... It really hurt to hear him say those words. I don't know how much I cried, but it all just came out because I kept hearing his words repeat over and over in my head." He nodded understandingly.

"Why didn't you call me?" he asked sincerely. I thought for a moment. Why didn't I call him? I took a deep breath, unsure of what to say.

"I'm not sure... I guess I just decided to be a big girl for once. You've become my hero, my safe place... but I just don't want to become so dependent on you that I feel like I need you to hold my hand all the time. It was hard to do... But I think it was necessary."

He looked at me with a bright expression. A beautiful smile grew on his face. He bit his bottom lip, slightly, and nodded. Everything about this man was beautiful to me. Obviously, he was always attractive to me because I dated him; but there was something about him these days that made him more attractive. His spirit outshined his physical features, and while I still wasn't quite used to that, I very much liked it.

The rest of lunch was great. We caught up on each other's past week's adventures. By the end of our meal, we both were pretty full, so we decided to head back to the school. As always, he walked me to my room.

"Thanks for lunch," I said with a small smile. He chuckled.

"You know I gotchu." A light giggle fell from my lips. He looked into my eyes with a soft expression on his face. I quickly glanced at his lips as he licked them. Being around him was becoming more and more difficult being that we were just friends at the moment. He slowly wrapped his arms around my waist and pulled me closer to him. My breath quickened as I contemplated what he was about to do. He pulled me into his chest and hugged me tightly. I exhaled slightly disappointed, silently cursing myself for even thinking he was going to kiss me.

"I really missed you this past week," he said breaking me out of my thoughts. I smiled into his chest. I stood on my tippy toes and planted a soft kiss on his cheek.

"I missed you, too." He smiled warmly as we stared at one another. He bit his bottom lip like he did last time but looked away.

"A'ight. I should go. I have some homework to do. Let's get up later, though." I nodded.

"Okay. See you later." He let me out of his strong embrace, and I turned to walk in my suite. I looked back at him as he stood with a conflicted expression. I waved one last time before closing the door. He waved and disappeared behind the door.

I turned my back to the door and put my face in my hands.

Why didn't I just kiss him? I don't know how much longer I can just be friends with him. I swear Chris Brown's "Should've Kissed You" could have started playing.

Suddenly there was a knock on the door startling me. I frowned and opened the door without checking to see who it was. To my surprise, Anthony was standing there.

"Anthony... Is everything okay?" I asked concerned. He stepped closer and closer until our bodies were almost touching. He softly held my face with his strong hands and stared deep into my eyes. Thoughts swam through my head. Although I knew what was about to happen, I couldn't wrap my brain around it. His eyes flickered from my eyes to my lips repeatedly. Being this close to him and inhaling his scent was making everything around me hazy. My eyes got lower and lower as he leaned his head closer.

"I don't know if I can go any longer without kissin' you, Kyrah," he said lowly. His deep voice sent chills through my body.

"M-me n-neither..." I stuttered. He slowly exhaled and softly pressed his lips to mine. He lightly kissed me, and I kissed back without any hesitation. This kiss was unlike the first time we kissed last year. This one was very gentle. Almost in desperation and longing from the both of us. We had both been keeping in emotions and feelings for one another all this time. We both had been waiting for this to happen. At that moment, that kiss made me forget everything I had experienced.

It was as if all the hurt and pain didn't even matter. The butterflies I felt every time I was around him multiplied by one hundred.

Our lips finally parted after an eternity of bliss, but our bodies were still touching. His warm embrace made me feel safe as I looked into his eyes. He gave me one last peck before he slowly backed away. My stomach dropped because I didn't want him to move. I exhaled as he stared at me.

"My fault," he apologized, "I couldn't help myself. It just seemed like the right time..." He looked down before quickly looking back at me to see my reaction. I couldn't speak. All I could think about was kissing him again. I stepped closer to him closing the gap between us. I stood on my tippy toes, softly grabbing the back of his head with both my hands, and softly pressed my lips against his. He kissed me back, but it was almost as if he was restraining himself. Before we both could deepen the kiss, he stopped and looked down. I frowned.

"What's wrong?" I asked, confused and still slightly dazed.

"Nun'... I just don't want us to go too far. I don't want us to repeat our past mistakes."

"Oh..." was all I could say.

Okay, now we really swapped places. I want it, but now he's against it. What is going on with me?

I sighed in frustration. I wasn't in the least bit frustrated with him but with myself. I couldn't stop imagining him in a way that I knew wasn't right. That kiss unlocked some thoughts and physical emotions that I worked hard to get rid of. He grabbed one of my hands and smirked.

"Kyrah, believe me when I say I've been thinkin' about and wantin' to kiss your lips. I don't regret it. I just don't want to compromise or make you compromise." I nodded in understanding, still trying to keep my thoughts from going left. The images of him kissing me and holding me just wouldn't get out of my head. He leaned in and kissed me softly on the forehead.

"I gotta go. I'll see you later," he said before releasing my hand. I nodded.

"Okay. See you..." He smiled and walked away, leaving me with my thoughts.

"Alana, I have a serious problem," I told my best friend over Face-Time. I hadn't realized it had been a hot minute since we last talked. So much was going on with me, it didn't occur to me that I was shutting those closest to me out.

"Uh oh. What's going on?" she asked. Her face expressed concern but also showed that she was curious to see what I had to say. I sighed deeply.

"It's Anthony... He and I are like best friends these days. He kissed me today and I'm feeling things... I like him again, but these feelings are more physical. Like, I really want him." I facepalmed to avoid her eyes on my iPhone screen.

"Kyrah..."

"I know, I know. It's not like it will happen, anyway."

She frowned slightly. "What do you mean 'it won't happen'?"

I began chewing my bottom lip a little thinking of how much Anthony had changed since Alana last heard about him. She of all people knew how much turmoil I went through in my relationship with him, and honestly, I know a lot of people would actually disapprove of our new-found friendship. But to be honest, there was nothing anybody could say or do that would make me not be his friend anymore. If anything, he has been the only one that was consistent throughout all I've been dealing with.

"Well...," I finally responded, "He's a legit Christian now. Actually, he's like a disciple. Like he's so different, we completely swapped places. He's been here encouraging me, speaking over me, praying for me, sending me Bible Verses, inviting me to church, all that. He's actually what I wish I could be again..." I drifted off into my thoughts again until Alana spoke up.

"Wow, girl. So, you're okay with being friends with him? Even after everything?"

I shrugged. "Yeah. I need him as a friend right now. He's been here this whole time. Who he is now completely erased who he was last year. I want him in my life." She smirked and looked away for a second. She looked back at me with a full smile.

"You're in love." I blushed.

"Maybe... But we can't be together, yet. It's not time."

She nodded. "Maybe not... But it'll happen. Something tells me that this friendship is the foundation for something greater."

After I hung up with Alana, I sat and thought about what she said. Part of me was still thinking about how I wanted Anthony physically, but I chopped it up to me just being insanely attracted to this new person he is. The more I thought about Anthony, the more I wanted to talk to him. I specifically wanted to talk to him about wanting to sleep with him, but I wasn't sure if it would make him uncomfortable or not. Rolling my eyes, I lay down and dozed into a nap from thinking so much.

Chapter Twelve

I paced back and forth in my living room mentally preparing myself to talk to Anthony. This was an awkward conversation that I didn't really want to have, but I felt like I should have it with him.

Just lay it all on the table, Kyrah...

I jumped at the sound of a knock on the door. It had been a few hours since our kiss and the thought of being around him filled my stomach with butterflies. After taking a few deep breaths, I opened the door. He looked at me and smiled his gorgeous smile. My heartbeat quickened. I felt like I did when I first saw him last year.

"Hey, beautiful," he greeted me as he pulled me in for a hug.

"Hi," I said softly as I melted in his arms. He released me and we walked to the couch.

"So, what's up? You good?" he asked looking at me. I nodded and smiled a little while trying to find some words.

"Yep. Everything's great... Just great." *Why am I being so awkward?* I exhaled slowly making eye contact with him. He was staring at me with a smirk.

"Something's botherin' you. What's up, Kyrah? Be real." He chuckled while still looking at me.

Here goes nothing. "Well, I have to kind of put this out there because I don't want things to be weird between us. Anthony, that kiss earlier... I have been waiting for you to do that, but I didn't expect it to unlock some old feelings that I stored away. What I'm saying is, I am very, very, *very* attracted to you."

He frowned a little and laughed deeply. "I'm attracted to you, too, Kyrah." I sighed in frustration knowing that he didn't understand what I really meant.

"No, Anthony. I mean I'm really attracted to you... Like physically." His facial expression suddenly changed and revealed that he understood. He smiled a little and bit his bottom lip. I blushed and looked down at my lap.

"You gotta stop looking at me like that..." I said aloud almost in a whisper. I silently began wishing I had kept that to myself.

"My bad. A'ight, we're both obviously very attracted to each other, but since we know that that's all the more reason for us to take it slow. I know last year I didn't make it easy for you because I didn't fully understand your choice to wait until marriage, and I am genuinely sorry for that. Every day I spend with you, I'm hoping to make up for all the ways I've hurt you. I'ma be completely honest with you: I want you. You have no idea. But I know now that you deserve so much more than a moment of pleasure. And I also don't want to put you in situations where you feel like you have to compromise.

"I know you're getting back on track with God. I want to help make sure you keep doing that. I want to be your accountability partner, your friend, eventually your boyfriend again, and your husband in the future. I wanna be your person, Kyrah. I want us both to grow together."

As he finished talking, I could feel my heart smiling. The peace I was searching for when we first dated settled into my heart at that very moment. Knowing that he wanted to take things slow and respected me and my body made the love I once felt deepen. I smiled at him and nodded.

"Okay," I finally responded. He returned the smile before standing up. He held out one of his hands for me to grab. I placed my hand safely in his and stood up to face him.

"Kyrah," he began looking into my eyes, "will you do me the honor of goin' on an official redo first date with me next Sunday?"

A small giggle fell from my lips. "I would love to, Anthony."

"Bet. Well, I'ma go. I didn't even get to do any homework earlier because I ended up falling asleep. I'll come see you tomorrow, a'ight?" I glanced down and he was still holding my hand. I smiled before looking back at him.

"Sounds good. See you tomorrow," I responded. He bent down and kissed me sweetly on the cheek. Feeling the blush coming on, I looked down at my feet. After he walked out the door, I collapsed on the couch replaying everything in my head...

***

One week later

Hectic. That's the best way to describe my room right now. I searched and searched for something to wear on this date with Anthony. He said we would be going somewhere after church, but after spending the week playing catch up and preparing for finals, this date was the last thing on my mind. Catching up in all my classes was draining and made me regret skipping in the first place. On top of that, I've been doing some homework for Moriah. As much as I wanted to put all my focus on this date, I couldn't. I sighed, as I continued to search through my drawers and closet for something decent to wear. Part of me knew that Anthony really didn't care what I wore, but the other part of me still wanted to make a good impression since it was a "first date redo".

A soft knock on my door broke me out of my misery. I walked to the door and opened it to find Raynah standing there. A small smile grew on my face.

"Hey," I said before turning back to my chaotic room.

"Woah. What happened in here?" she asked with a light laugh. I groaned.

"I have a date after church, and I can't find anything to wear. I think I'm thinking about it too much."

She frowned and looked at me like I was crazy. "What?" I asked.

"A date? With who?" I hesitated for a second carefully reading her face.

"Anthony..." I answered exasperated. I was in no mood to answer questions; I just wanted to find the perfect appropriate outfit for church and this date. Raynah smiled warmly.

"Aw. I always loved you guys together. Well, let's find something to wear." I smiled, silently thanking her for not hounding me and being supportive.

With Raynah's help, I was finally able to decide on a pair of high-waisted blue skinny jeans, a dark gray long-sleeved body suit to wear under, and a long gray cardigan. I finished this outfit off with some gray low heel over-the-knee boots. After putting on my outfit, I refreshed the curls of my afro and put on some pearl earrings. I stared into the mirror wondering if I needed anything else. I didn't feel like bothering with any makeup other than mascara, so I decided that I didn't need to add anything extra.

As I finished up the last bit of my look, there was a knock on the door. Raynah left my room and went to answer it. I heard the calm of Anthony's voice and my stomach immediately filled with butterflies. I heard his footsteps approaching my room. I looked away from the mirror to meet him face-to-face.

"Hey," he greeted with a warm smile. He walked towards me with an amused expression after looking at the disaster in my room. "You look beautiful."

My face burned with blush. "Thank you... I'm ready to go when you are." He nodded. I grabbed my purse, Bible, and phone. He held out his hand for me to grab and I eagerly took hold of it.

Church pretty much flew by since the sermon was shorter than last time. Anthony and I were on our way to start our date and I couldn't have been more at peace. I wasn't nervous like our first date, rather, I was eager. I was truly excited about spending this time with him other than as friends.

We pulled up into a small parking lot full of cars. The thought of being around a large crowd made me nervous, but I didn't want him to think I didn't want to go on this date anymore. I took silent deep breaths as he parked the car. He looked over at me with soft eyes.

"Okay, so there's an art festival in town. I wasn't sure if you wanted to go because it's so many people here. I know being around large crowds has been difficult for you, and I won't force you. I'll be with you the whole time, but if that still doesn't make you comfortable, I have a backup plan for our date." He smiled a little waiting for me to respond.

All the nerves I felt suddenly disappeared. I smiled warmly at him.

"I'm down for this."

"You sure?" he asked with a smile forming on his lips. I nodded and returned the smile. We got out of the car and walked towards the festival hand-in-hand.

We spent a few hours walking around, people-watching, and joking around. No matter how much time we spend together, it's never a dull moment. After we finally decided we were over the festival, Anthony planned for us to walk to a nearby café. Once we were seated, we got into a deep conversation.

"So, how do you feel about all of this? Us, I mean," he asked before taking a sip of his soda. I sat and thought about my answer. The thing is, I knew I wanted to be with him again. I always knew that our breakup wouldn't be a forever thing, but I wasn't expecting us to become close under these circumstances.

"I know I want to be with you. I'm just not sure if I'm ready, yet. But I know that this is happening..." I paused, "Honestly, I should've known the way you kept popping up after we broke up last year." We shared a quick laugh.

"True. But I know you're not ready. I'm not trying to jump into anything or make you jump into anything. I personally think your heart needs a break... y'know, some time to heal. My desire and goal are to pursue you, to court you. I don't care how long it takes because I know you're the one for me. I'm enjoying this friendship and I want this to continue. I want us to take our time this go 'round. Really get to know each other. God will let us both know when it's time for us to take that next step in our relationship. A'ight?" I smiled a smile that matched the smile on my heart.

I took in everything he said before taking a sip of my lemonade. Our food came shortly after, and we continued some small talk. This date was far better than the first date we originally had. Everything was easy this time around and I felt comfortable. I felt comfortable knowing that he wanted to truly be with me for me. We didn't want the date to end just yet, so we bought some time by ordering dessert.

I looked Anthony in his eyes. "When did you know I was the one?" He returned my gaze and slowly licked his lips, contemplating his answer. I took this opportunity to take in his appearance. *This man is beyond fine. His locs are endless. His shimmering brown eyes are singing a song of love to my heart.*

"I knew for sure when I saw you with Jesse the day after your birthday." I frowned slightly caught off guard. He nodded answering my unspoken question of assurance.

"I remember being so angry and hurt that day. All I could think was 'Another dude is with my wife. How could God let that happen?' Granted, I was foolin' around with Erica again which in itself is hypocritical… But I was just so hurt that day. Like a piece of me had been stolen. I was angry at God because He let everything between us fall apart. I thought that everything would be easygoing between us after I got saved.

I remember asking Him why He didn't care about me. That feeling lasted until I got home for the summer. I found myself hitting up a buncha girls. One night before I was about to go sleep with one of them, my grandma called me." A single tear floated down his cheek. "She said 'God is about to move in your life. He loves you and He wants to heal your heart. He is calling you. You have to yield to His calling. The woman you love is your wife, but she is waiting for you. You have to let God change your heart and work in your life.'

I remember crying my eyes out that night. That night…," he sniffed, "changed me forever. I'm forever grateful for God using my grandma. I surrendered everything to God and He graciously transformed me." I was slightly taken aback at the sight of him getting a little emotional, but I also understood. I reached my hand across the table for him to grab. He placed one hand in mine while he used the other to quickly wipe his eyes.

"Wow. Anthony, I had no idea... Maybe that's why Jesse and I just ended so abruptly." I responded. He smiled.

"Maybe... But I was gon' wait for you no matter what... no matter how long it took."

My heart smiled and my eyes got a little glossy. He intertwined our fingers.

"Can't believe you got me cryin' up in here," he joked. I giggled and shrugged.

"It's okay. It only made me feel closer to you... I just thank God for this transformation and Him using your grandma to speak over you when you really needed it... He truly does come through when you need Him to."

"No doubt about it. He truly is amazing. I never saw myself here a year ago... but I'm so glad to be here. He has changed my life so much," he responded. Who would've thought that we would be praising God together after everything we had been through?

"The last time I saw you this emotional was last year," I said. He chuckled. I wiped the tears that stained his cheek and stared into his eyes.

"I know, right?" I smirked and nodded. He smiled as he gazed into my eyes. My stomach filled with butterflies as I stared back into his. A happy sigh fell from his lips. He reached for my other hand and held both of them so gently. He kissed them tenderly.

"I love you, Kyrah."

My heart rate accelerated as a smile grew on my face. "I love you, too."

Chapter Thirteen

After Anthony and I got back to the school, he walked me to my room like he always does. I spent the rest of the afternoon cleaning my room after my earlier disaster. It took me way too long to put everything back in its place and organize it the way I had it. I made a mental note to just narrow it down to three outfits next time. A light knock on my door caught my attention as I was hanging up one of my jackets.

"Come in," I called out softly. The door slowly opened, and Raynah's head popped in.

"Hey, girl," she greeted as she walked all the way in. She sat in the bean bag chair in the corner. "How was your date?" I felt my cheeks get hot and I suppressed my smile as much as I could. I faced her and shrugged.

"It was nice." Her face fell and she scoffed.

"Just nice? Kyrah, don't BS me. Be for real, for real. How was it?" My smile betrayed me, and I laughed a little.

"It was amazing," I gushed. She jumped and ran over to me. She grabbed my hands and pulled me towards my bed, both of us plopping down at the same time.

"Give me the details!" I told her everything. This would be a day I would never get tired of talking about because of how Anthony made me feel. Her smile grew with every word that came from my mouth.

"Kyrah, any man that cries is a real man," she said giggling. I laughed and nodded.

"I definitely agree with that. It was such a nice day, though. I really enjoyed his company, and he just treated me with such care. He's so different now. At first, I wasn't so sure he had really changed, but his actions, even the way he talks to me and how he dresses and walks have changed. I have fallen in love with him all over again but for a different reason." Raynah looked at me puzzled. A slight frown grew on her face.

"What reason?"

I smiled. "The Jesus in him."

***

After talking to Raynah, I decided to take a much-needed nap. Once I woke up, I fought the idea of working on some homework, but eventually caved since I still had some catching up to do before the semester ended. An hour into it, I started to get a little restless, so I took a break and decided to go walk outside around the small campus.

The sun was starting to set for the evening and the scenery of the campus at this time was absolutely beautiful. As I was passing by the field, I found some benches and sat on one of them. A small sigh fell from my lips as I watched the sun set over the soccer field.

"It's beautiful, isn't it?" I heard a familiar male voice getting closer. I looked up and saw Sean walking towards me. A smile grew on my face.

"Hey, Sean!" I stood up and gave him a big hug once he approached me. He embraced me and chuckled.

"Long time, no see, huh?" he said as we let go of each other. I laughed a little.

"Yeah, sorry about that. It's been... rough, to say the least." We both sat on our regular bench and stared at the sun making its way down for the evening. He looked at me, giving a small smile.

"I heard... Don't sweat it, though. You needed your time and space. But don't forget that I'm always here for you, a'ight? You're one of my favorite people so I really care about you. I'm glad you're getting better, though." My heart warmed at his words. I smiled and nudged him with my shoulder.

"Thanks, Sean. I appreciate it."

"Any time, sis."

Sean and I caught up for a while until we both decided to call it and go back to the dorms. I found out he was staying in another building, so we had to part ways. As I was walking back to my building, I heard footsteps jogging behind. I did my best to remain calm and keep my anxiety down so I wouldn't let this unknown person know I was afraid. As the footsteps grew closer, my heart began to beat so fast I thought it would jump out of my chest. Suddenly I felt strong, yet familiar arms grab my waist and pull me close. A small scream came from my lips.

"Woah, babygirl. It's me," Anthony said laughing a little. I sighed in relief and held one hand to my chest to calm down. Anthony slowly turned me around so I could face him.

"Why did you do that?" I said breathlessly with a small laugh. I playfully hit him on the chest. He chuckled lightly, pulling me closer to him, making me blush. My eyes slowly dragged to my feet.

"What you doin' out here?" he asked. I met his gaze and saw him focusing on me. I shrugged.

"Needed to get out of my room. Started to feel restless so I watched the sunset." He smiled and leaned in, planting a quick, sweet kiss on my forehead.

"Well, let's get you back inside." He unwrapped his arms from around my waist and we walked inside our dorm.

After arriving at my suite, we decided to chill out in my room for a while. We both sat on my bed, my back against the headboard, my feet in his lap and his back on the wall. We talked and laughed for hours like we hadn't just hung out earlier that day. Somehow in the process of running our mouths, we ended up cuddling. After a while, it became silent, and Anthony sat up.

"It's late, I should head back to my room." I sat up and nodded.

"Yeah, we should call it a night. Thanks for hanging out with me." He smiled and bit his bottom lip slightly.

"Any time." He stared at me, and I took the time to admire him. We'd already established that we were going to take things slow, but I could already see I was falling deep. He ran his fingers through the curls of my afro and smiled.

"I've been meaning to tell you that I love the highlights and the nose piercing. They look beautiful on you." Speechless, I looked down and smiled a little.

"Oh, thanks." He placed his hand under my chin, making me look at him. He started inching closer to me. He leaned in and kissed me on the corner of my mouth.

"Before I go, I wanna ask you somethin'." Thoughts swam through my head. Unsure of what was going to come out of his mouth, I nodded, losing my breath due to the closed space between us.

"Will you have lunch with me tomorrow?" He smiled and chuckled. I laughed softly.

"I would love to, Anthony." I pulled him into an embrace, feeling him breathe deeply. He returned the embrace, hugging me tight as if he was going to lose me. I didn't want this moment to end. I learned that being in his arms was one of my favorite things in the world. He began to loosen his grip and I sighed.

Once Anthony left, I reminisced about how close we were. I touched the corner of my mouth where he left a sweet kiss. One thing was for sure, I wanted him in every aspect. But I also remember how I felt last year when we first slept together. Sex was something I always imagined to be magical. I always prided myself in knowing that I was going to wait until my wedding night to give my body to the only man who would ever see and feel it. But everything changed last year, including the way I viewed sex altogether. After sleeping with both Anthony and Jesse twice each, my understanding of what God created sex to be was completely clouded.

Sex had become something that was a temporary fix for me. It became harder to resist. When the opportunity presented itself, it was hard for me to walk away. Now, I would inch closer and closer to doing it, testing myself to see if I could stop before it was too late. But with Anthony being so different these days, sleeping with him didn't seem like it was going to happen, which I was halfway thankful for.

I finally stopped thinking long enough to change into my pajamas and lay down. My brain was still wrapped around Anthony and how badly I physically wanted him. A sigh fell from my lips as my eyes grew heavy. *Is this really who I've become? I guess if it's not one thing, it's another, huh? I've changed into a completely different person in a matter of a year.* After thinking for a few more minutes, I finally drifted into a deep sleep...

***

"Kyrah, I don't know if I can fight this anymore," Anthony said looking me dead in my eyes. We were sitting on the couch, one of his hands caressing one of my thighs. I bit my lip as I looked at his hand.

"I don't think I can either." He smirked as he grabbed both of my hands. He stood up, gently pulling me with him. Never breaking eye contact, he slowly leaned down as if he was going to kiss me softly.

"I want you," he whispered against my lips. I tried to speak words, but nothing would come out. Suddenly, his head dipped, and I felt his lips touch the skin on my neck. I sighed knowing where this was headed. This is something I'd been wanting desperately, but I couldn't shake the feeling of guilt. He slowly trailed kisses up to my jaw and then to my lips. I kissed back instantly without holding back.

After a few moments, the door of my suite opened interrupting us.

It was...

"Anthony?" I asked confused.

"Kyrah, I don't wanna do this. Not yet." I frowned, even more puzzled by what was happening. I was standing here in the arms of Anthony, only he was standing at the door. I looked up at the man holding me, who no longer

> *looked like Anthony, but a body full of lust. I fearfully*
> *backed away and looked towards the door. The real An-*
> *thony was standing there staring at me in desperation.*
>
> *I tried to move my feet to run towards the door, but*
> *it felt like my feet were suddenly glued to the floor. Tears*
> *rolled down my cheeks as the lust-filled body moved closer*
> *to me. I closed my eyes hoping it would disappear.*

My eyes shot open, and my heart was racing as if it was going to jump out of my chest. As I sat up in my bed, I could feel the cold sweat dripping down my back. I looked around my dark room before checking my phone to see what time it was. *2:00 a.m.* I sighed deeply trying to calm my racing heart.

That dream frightened me, to say the least. But I knew it was only a symbol of the large amount of lust I was feeling for Anthony. And truth be told, I really wasn't sure what to do about it. I didn't really know who to talk to about it. Partially because I was embarrassed; the other reason was that I didn't really know how I could put it into words. I also couldn't deny that the more time I spent with Anthony made me want him more. But I knew that I had to keep this desire under control. The last thing I wanted was to make him feel the way I felt last year. I couldn't imagine putting him in the same position.

I slowly shook my head and grabbed my phone. Despite my embarrassment, I knew I had to talk to somebody. I quickly shot Moriah a text asking her if she could see me in the afternoon. I knew she wouldn't respond since she was obviously asleep, so I put my phone on Do Not Disturb and lay back down, eventually dozing back off into a deep sleep.

I woke up around 9:00 a.m. to the sound of music blasting from outside my window.

Really? It's too early. And it's Monday! I thought to myself.

Suddenly thoughts from my dream last night swam through my head as I stared at the ceiling. Then thoughts about how Anthony and I spent time together last night took over and a small smile grew on my face. I checked my phone and saw his name on my screen indicating that he'd sent me a text.

> Good morning, beautiful. I gotta work after my last class this afternoon, but I'll do my best to come see you this evening. If not, I'll definitely call you. I hope you have a great day. Do something productive. Don't sit in that room all day, lol. See you later, babygirl.

The smile that was already plastered on my face grew larger as my eyes scanned over the heartfelt message repeatedly. A deep breath arose in my chest as I sat up to get my day started. I took a hot, thoughtful shower and got dressed shortly after. Once I finished styling my hair in a puff and finishing the rest of my hygiene routines, I checked my phone to see if Moriah had responded to my text. I silently thanked God when I saw that she could see me around 11:00. Seeing that it was 10:30, I figured I'd better hurry up and head to the church.

The drive there was silent. Normally I'd have music playing, but I had a lot on my mind. It seemed as if I kept having problem after problem. First the battle with depression, and now my strong desire to be with Anthony physically. My mind wondered on memories of what his skin felt like on mine, and how it felt having our bodies close together. I quickly shook my head of those thoughts and groaned in frustration.

"Lord, help me."

I finally pulled up to the church and parked the car. I walked in, greeted the secretary, and hurried to Moriah's office. I softly knocked on the door and she looked from her computer with a big smile.

"There's my girl. Hey, Kyrah," she greeted excitedly. I returned the smile.

"Hey, Moriah." I walked into the office and made myself comfortable on the couch. She grabbed her notebook and sat beside me instead of sitting in the chair across from me like she normally does.

"Okay, so you texted me in the wee hours of the night and admittedly, that made me worry a little. Are you okay?" she asked sincerely.

I nodded unsurely. "I guess so." She studied me and cocked her head to the side, her whole body facing me.

"So, what's going on, then?"

My mind was a battle by this point, and I was unsure how to word what's been going on. How do I explain to someone that I am struggling to stop lusting after the man I love but can't have at this very moment?

"Well," I began. "I keep having these thoughts about Anthony that I almost feel like I can't control. And to be honest, it's really taking a toll on me right now."

"Okay, what kind of thoughts?"

I bit my bottom lip and looked down in shame. *Do I really have to say it out loud?*

"Are you scared to lose him? Scared he hasn't changed?" she continued to press.

I shook my head. "No, neither of those. I'm too embarrassed to say." We sat silently as she thought about what it could be. After a moment of silence, she chuckled.

"Kyrah, are you having thoughts about sleeping with him?" I sighed in relief and looked up at her. My whole body relaxed knowing that I didn't have to say it.

"Yes," I finally responded.

She chuckled some more. "Kyrah, that is normal. And I can understand why you're embarrassed. But I'm assuming it's a little deeper than what you're telling me since you hit me up. What is really concerning you about this?"

I hesitantly began telling her about the dream and how much it scared me. I know that it was just a dream, but it felt so real. And I knew that I needed to get this under some kind of control. Once I finished talking, I felt a bit of relief and was ready to receive whatever advice she had for me.

"That's pretty interesting," she said after I finished.

"What should I do? The last thing I want to do is make Anthony feel the way I felt last year. He's so different now and I just feel like we've completely swapped places. It has been so hard keeping my mind from going left and I don't know how much longer I'll be able to stop it."

A loving, gracious smile spread across her face.

"Kyrah, first I want you to understand that the desire to have sex is not a bad thing nor is it a sin. If it were, God wouldn't have given us that innate desire to be with someone in that way. It's honestly just how you go about it. You and Anthony have both made some mistakes, but the beauty in your relationship is that you both are working to move past those mistakes. And I know for certain he is fighting the same internal battle as you if not, probably worse. My advice for you both would be to really sit, talk about these feelings you're having for one another, and come to some mutual boundaries. And once you create those boundaries, you have to respect them. If there is something that might cause him to stumble, don't do it, and vice versa. But I promise you, we all experience it. All you have to do is just ask the Holy Spirit to take over your mind, so you don't lust because then that'll definitely lead you to fall."

I nodded as I took in her words. Anthony and I were both strangers to boundaries at this point, so I tried to come up with some on the spot. But I was having trouble pinning specific things because these days, everything about him made me want him. The way he walks, the way he smiles, his voice, how he always looks me in the eyes when he's talking to me, how he hugs me—everything.

"Don't stress yourself out. Think about it and then talk to Anthony, okay?" Moriah said after moments of silence.

"Okay. Thanks, Moriah. I really appreciate it. I should get going. I have class soon." We both stood up and she hugged me tightly. We said our goodbyes and I headed out of the church.

***

Class was dragging by so slowly and it was even worse because Anthony was having a busy workday so we couldn't text while I sat here. This World Literature class had its interesting moments, but for the most part, my teacher was a sarcastic man who only enjoyed talking about himself. He also liked to make us write two-page papers after every class session which was a bit much for me considering I had just finished catching up on all his assignments after missing classes. However, I was grateful that he didn't really care about attendance and was willing to work with me so I wouldn't fail.

After another thirty minutes of just listening to him talk about himself, he finally dismissed us, and I quickly packed my book bag and headed out of the classroom. I walked swiftly hoping to avoid the large crowd that was due to fill up the lawn for a midday event. As I was exiting the building, I spotted Jesse talking to some girl. A light chuckle escaped my mouth as I rolled my eyes. *What a dog...* I placed my hand on the door to walk out when I heard him call my name. I exhaled trying to control the attitude I felt trying to take over my body.

"Yoooo, Kyrah," he said as he approached me. I looked up at him with a straight face.

"What, Jesse?"

"Where ya headed?" A smile formed on his face.

"Why?" I asked trying to contain the attitude I could feel rising in my chest. This was one of those moments I wish Anthony could come swooping in to save me like he's been doing lately. The smile on Jesse's face disappeared as he saw the expression I wore.

"I was wondering' if you had time to finish hearin' me out? I just really want you to understand."

I frowned in disbelief. "Jesse, I told you already that I don't even want to listen to anything else you have to say. What you did was inexcusable. You really hurt me. But I forgive you, okay? And I would really just like to go on with my life."

He nodded as he shoved his hands in his pockets. I studied his face as he contemplated what to say next. I sighed and softened my facial expression as I felt my attitude fading.

"Look, Jesse. I just need some space. I can't move on if you keep trying to talk to me about why you did what you did. It doesn't matter anymore. I'm over it. I don't want to live in the past. What we had was nice at the time, but it's over now. Let's both just move forward and go on with our lives."

A half smile appeared on his lips, and he nodded.

"I understand, Kyrah. I'll respect your wishes and give you your space. I just really want you to know how sorry I really am. I never intended to hurt you, for real."

I shrugged. "Don't worry about it. Like I said, I forgive you."

"So, we good?"

I nodded and gave an inauthentic smile.

"Yeah, I guess..."

I left him standing there with nothing else to say, but with a brain full of conflicted thoughts.

Chapter Fourteen

The next few weeks flew by and before I knew it, it was time to go home for Christmas break. Thankfully I'd managed to pull my grades up enough to pass my classes and make up for the classes that I'd missed. I sat on my bed staring at my phone, watching the time tick by. After having that conversation with Jesse a few weeks back, I realized how much hatred I was carrying in my heart. But because I chose to start letting the hurt go and move on, I've been able to open myself back up to Anthony, my best friends, and my roommates. A deep sigh rose in my chest as I looked at my packed suitcase. My mind began to wonder just what this break had in store for me.

Just as I was getting lost in my train of thought, my phone began vibrating repeatedly, bringing me back to reality. A small smile immediately formed on my lips at the sight of Anthony's name.

"Hello?" I answered the phone, putting the call on the speaker setting.

"Hey, babygirl. You all packed up?" His deep voice floated through the speaker on my phone, and I could feel my heart flutter in reaction.

"Yep. I'm just sitting here waiting for you." His deep, hearty chuckle filled my ears, pulling a small giggle out of me.

"I promise I am knocking on your door in the next thirty seconds."

I bit my bottom lip slightly, nodding.

"Okay. I'll be waiting." We hung up the phone and just as he promised, there was a knock on my door as soon as the call ended. I went to open the door and as I did, I could feel my breath being taken away just at the sight of him. He had his locs pulled back in a messy low bun and his glasses on with a pair of Nike joggers and a plain black T-shirt.

"Hey, mama. You ready?" he asked smiling. I smiled softly in return and nodded.

"Yep. All ready to go."

Anthony offered to come with me to Augusta so he could finally meet my family. Although he would only be staying the first couple of days of the break due to him having to come back for work, he expressed how he really wanted to spend some time with me away from the school setting. I appreciated this gesture and truthfully, it only did the obvious which made me fall even deeper in love with him.

He grabbed my suitcase, and I grabbed my phone, keys, and small backpack. We headed out of my suite, quietly enjoying one another's company. As we approached my car, he stopped behind the trunk.

"Everything okay?" I asked.

He smirked, "Yeah. I'm just a little nervous about meeting your people. I mean, do they know everything that happened between us? What if they don't like me?" The smirk on his face disappeared and he closed his eyes as he looked up to the sky.

"Bruh," he continued, "what if your dad flips? Especially after everything I put you through last year." He began pacing slightly, and I couldn't contain the giggles that rose in my chest. "Like, it ain't like we datin' or nothin', yet, but still. I'm finna meet your folks, and if they already hate me from last year, ain't no comin' back from that, man. Plus—"

I laughed and moved closer to him. I placed a hand on his shoulder, and he stopped, looking me deep in the eyes. His eyes showed genuine anxiety and I could tell he was really battling his nervousness inside. A warm, reassuring smile grew on my face, and I watched his whole demeanor relax.

"Anthony don't worry. My mom is the only person that knows about you and she's excited to meet you. My family is going to love you. And like you said, we're not dating, yet. So, if they meet you as my friend and like you, then you're already in the family. Relax." I smiled and planted a kiss on his cheek.

He exhaled slowly, nodding his head in response. A low "you right" came from his lips and he smiled. He moved closer, gently grabbing my waist as he leaned in to plant a sweet kiss on my forehead. He proceeded to place my bags in the trunk for me and opened the driver-side door for me to get in. I started my car and waited for him to get in his so he could follow me on this road trip. After he made sure he had everything he needed, I drove out of the parking lot with him following behind.

After driving for two and a half hours, Anthony and I finally arrived at my house. I got out of the car and waited for Anthony to get out of his. As he made his way closer to me, I could see the worry on his face that he failed to hide. I grabbed one of his hands and gently squeezed it.

"Hey," I said trying to get him to snap out of his obsessive thoughts. He looked at me, frowning slightly. "Relax, please."

He chuckled nervously, "I'm trying to. I need a minute."

I smirked and shook my head.

"Boy, come on." With his hand still in mine, I pulled him to follow me in the house. After I unlocked the door, I gave him a quick reassuring glance and proceeded to walk inside.

"There she is!" I heard my dad say from the living room. As we walked further into the house, everyone gravitated towards us, surrounding us in love.

"You must be Anthony," my dad greeted. He playfully gave him a hard handshake and a fake stern face.

"Yes, sir."

My dad stared him down and I could see the sweat forming on Anthony's forehead. I suppressed the laugh that was building in my throat as I watched the exchange. After a few seconds of a hard stare-down, my dad laughed and let go of his hand.

"I'm just messing with you, man. It's nice to finally meet you, Anthony." Anthony sighed deeply and smiled.

"You too, Mr. Brown."

We all made ourselves comfortable in the family room and needless to say, Anthony fit right in. My family loved him. Watching everyone interact with him makes me wonder why we didn't do this when we were dating last year. I stared at him as he talked to my younger brother, Kyrie, and I could feel my heart leaping in my chest.

After everyone spent time getting to know Anthony for a few hours, they all went their separate ways, leaving us alone in the family room watching TV.

"Yo, your family is cool. Why you keep them from me?" he joked. I chuckled.

"I did not keep them from you. I just had to make sure you weren't going anywhere, first." He smirked and nodded.

"I can understand that. I'ma hate leaving you in a few days. I wish I could spend all my time with you." I shook my head and sighed.

"Nah. You'd get tired of me after a while."

A serious expression appeared on his face, and he frowned slightly. "Why you think that?"

I shrugged, "I know I can be a bit much at times. And you know I'm dealing with a lot. I'm surprised you're not tired of me now." I tried to joke it off, but I could tell what I said really shocked and bothered him. He scooted closer to me, never taking his eyes off mine. I could tell he was choosing his words carefully, something he seemed to do a lot nowadays. I tried my hardest not to get distracted by him and paid attention to the words that were forming on his lips. His lips. My Lord, this man did not understand the battle that was happening internally. *Keep it together, Kyrah. Remember, boundaries.*

"Kyrah, listen. I could never get tired of you. There may be moments in the future where we'll need to take some time apart because we all need some alone time. But tired of you? Nah. I could never. That don't even sound right coming from you. Don't think like that, a'ight, babygirl?"

I nodded taking in everything he said. He was right. I never got tired of him. I got tired of our drama, but even still, I would always want to be around him. I want to be around him all the time now.

"Okay. Well, since the conversation shifted... There's something I want to talk to you about." He squinted his eyes slightly as his expression became amused.

"Uh-oh. What happened? What I do?" I giggled and rolled my eyes.

"Nothing at all. I just wanted to talk to you about something that Moriah suggested we try. Setting boundaries."

He nodded, still with an unsure expression on his face.

"Set boundaries like how?" I explained what my session with Moriah was about. I told him about the dream, my feelings, and what I've been fighting against. Everything. Although I would've preferred to keep all of that to myself, I figured it was best to just lay everything on the table so that he would know exactly how I felt about him.

He chuckled slightly and nodded in agreement. He grabbed one of my hands and brought it to his soft lips. *Lord Jesus…*

"Okay—see. Like that. Don't do that. Please." He laughed and admitted that he was just trying to be sweet and reassure me, but promised he wouldn't do that again. We talked a little while longer about what boundaries we wanted to put in place so neither of us would tempt the other among many other things. That was one of my favorite things about us working on our friendship: we talked about everything under the sun and still had more to say. I loved moments like this. He made me feel as if nothing else mattered.

After another hour of running our mouths about random topics, we decided to call it a night. I showed him where the guest room was, and I headed to my room.

"Do you need anything before I go to my room?" He scanned the room briefly before looking at me and shook his head.

"Nah, I think I'm good." I nodded.

"Okay, cool. Well, I'm gonna go to bed. I'll see you in the morning?"

"Of course," he replied with a cute smirk. He gently grabbed my waist pulling me closer to him. He slowly leaned down and kissed my lips like he'd been waiting to do that all day. Truthfully, I'd been waiting all day for it. But I knew we needed to stop for numerous reasons. I slowly pulled away from the kiss and smirked.

"So much for boundaries, huh?" He joked. His arms were still around me and I rested my head on his chest.

"I know right?" I listened to his steady heartbeat and closed my eyes. I could've stayed like this forever, but I knew we couldn't. We said our final goodnights, and both headed to bed.

I woke up bright and early the next morning to the smell of breakfast. Knowing my mom, she was whipping up something since Anthony was here visiting. I decided to go ahead and get showered and dressed for the day. Not sure what the plan was for the day, I settled on a pair of joggers and a tank top. I sat on my bed and texted Anthony to see if he was awake, yet.

> Good morning, I think my mom is cooking a special breakfast since you're here. She's in rare form, lol. Would you like to explore the city today? I could show you around… (:

To my surprise, he responded within seconds. A smile formed on my lips as I read his reply.

> Yes. I can't wait. I woke up starving. We can definitely go ride around. I wanna know the place that raised my girl. (;

We texted back and forth until he said he was going to shower and put on some clothes. I headed to the kitchen to find my mom still cooking. The aroma of homecooked breakfast hit my nostrils with full force and my stomach began rumbling in response. I greeted my mom and sat down on one of the bar stools. Soon, everyone started to join us in the kitchen. I watched Anthony as he walked towards the kitchen, and he caught me staring. I blushed as he met my gaze and he smirked. He sat beside me and smiled.

"Morning, beautiful," he greeted.

"Morning, handsome."

We sat with my family and enjoyed breakfast as one big family. Later that day, Anthony and I went riding around just like we planned. We had a blast. I could tell he really enjoyed himself. It felt like he belonged there all this time. We decided to spend the day at the mall, checking out some new stores and some of my favorite local restaurants. And our night ended with a nice dinner, just the two of us. It was romantic and sweet. Something I was looking forward to doing more of with him.

With all the fun we were having together, the next day came, and our time together ended too soon. Before we both knew it, it was time for him to go back to Lawrenceville so he could go to work.

My family all gathered in the living room to say their goodbyes.

"Anthony, my man, it was really nice meeting you. We'd love to have you any time," my dad said as he gave him a handshake.

"Yeah, it feels like one of my kids is leaving," my mom chimed in. A smile grew on my face, and I let out a chuckle.

Anthony beamed, "Oh, I'll definitely be back. You guys are family now." We all laughed.

After everybody said goodbye, they dispersed leaving Anthony and me alone. Sadness settled in as it hit me that we wouldn't see each other for the next couple of weeks. He saw the look on my face and matched it. He forced himself to give a small smile. He grabbed one of my hands and brought it to his lips.

"I'm really gonna miss you… I wish I didn't have to leave or that you could come with me." I nodded.

"So, do I. But it's only a couple of weeks, right? And I know we'll talk to each other every day."

He chuckled, "Look at you. Looking at the bright side." I playfully rolled my eyes and laughed.

"Someone has to." We both stood in silence looking at each other. Neither of us wanting to say the words "goodbye".

He cleared his throat breaking eye contact. "I should get going so I can get enough rest for my shift in the morning."

I nodded, "Yeah, definitely…"

We walked to the door, him with his bags in his hands and me following closely behind him. I decided to walk him to his car just to savor every moment with him. After he put his bags in his backseat, he gently grabbed my hands and pulled me close to him. He wrapped his arms around me, and I rested my head on his chest. I did my very best to fight the tears that threatened to come out. I was admittedly really sad that he was leaving.

"Hey", he said grabbing my attention. I looked up at him and saw him staring at me. He smirked. He inched his face closer to mine and before I knew it, our lips touched. It's like our lips were magnetic and refused to stay away from each other. We both deepened the kiss as if we'd never have this opportunity again. We finally parted and he bit his bottom lip.

"I love you", he said looking me in my eyes.

I smiled, "I love you, too. I'll talk to you later."

"Bet. See you later." I backed away from him and watched as he got in the car. I stood in the driveway and waited for him to pull off. He gave me one last wave and a wink, backed out of the driveway, and headed down the street. I watched until he disappeared into the distance. A sigh fell from my lips as I stood there alone.

Chapter Fifteen

S pending time with my family was just what I needed to continue my healing process. Being home really reminded me how much I missed them. We did so much during my break. I got so lost in all of the excitement and fun that Christmas seemed to come so fast.

Like every year, we all stayed up on Christmas Eve and everyone opened one gift at midnight before we all went to bed. After we opened our gifts, watched a movie, and ate cookies, we all went to our rooms and headed to sleep. Around 12:30, Anthony called me which I expected since he got off so late.

"Hey, Merry Christmas, baby girl," he said as soon as his face appeared on the screen. One thing I was grateful for was FaceTime. We may not be able to be together physically, but it still felt like he was here.

I smiled and blushed, "Merry Christmas. You're off for the holiday?" He nodded and yawned.

"Yep, thank God. I'm so tired. I need the next few days off. I'm really looking forward to getting some rest."

"Yeah, you definitely need it." We carried on our conversation for a few more minutes until we both decided to call it a night.

For the next few days, I was able to talk to Anthony more which made me miss him more. Honestly, it felt like we were already dating even though we were just friends. We'd crossed our boundaries by sharing a few kisses here and there and truth be told, it has kind of blurred the lines for me. I'm not sure what we are at this point, but I'm enjoying it.

By the time New Year's rolled around, I was having mixed emotions. On one side, I was excited to get back to school to see everyone; however, I was sad because I would be leaving my family again. I know I could always come visit since they are just a drive away, but it wasn't the same.

My family and I were all sitting in the living room the weekend before I had to leave again.

"I'm going to miss you guys so much. I really enjoyed being home... and thank you guys for accepting Anthony so easily. He is a big part of my life right now," I said with a small smile on my face. Everyone nodded.

"Of course. He fit right in. You gotta bring him back one of these days," my brother, Kyrie said.

I chuckled, "I will, I promise."

Once I got back to school, everything and everyone picked up where we left it. I was so happy to see Tamra and Raynah again. We spent our first day back talking about how our breaks went. Tamra told us how her family spent their Christmas on a beach, which to be honest, sounds pretty nice. Raynah told us how she spent most of her break with her boyfriend, Tommy, which didn't surprise either of us.

"Okay", Tamra started, "enough about us. How was your break? How did it go with Anthony and your family?" They both sat on my bed with me eagerly waiting for my response. An instant blush appeared on my face that I couldn't even mask if I wanted to.

"Oh, they all love him so much. He just fit in so well. They told me I have to bring him back one day."

"Aww, our little Kyrah! Anthony met the folks! It's official-official", Raynah responded with a big smile.

I shrugged. "Ehh. Not exactly. Y'all, I still don't know if I'm ready to take that next step with him, yet", I admitted. Of course, I wanted to, but I really felt like there were still some unresolved feelings from last year in my heart.

Tamra frowned slightly, "What's holding you back?"

I shook my head, "I wish I knew..." was all I could muster up to say. They nodded understandingly not pushing the subject. We talked some more until we all decided to go our separate ways.

The rest of the day seemed to be pretty chill. Anthony was working so I knew I wouldn't get to see him until later that evening. I couldn't lie, I was excited to see him the most. It sucked that he couldn't stay the whole break with my family and me, but I was thankful that we got to see each other every day on campus.

Around 6:00 my phone lit up while I was finishing my unpacking. A smile grew on my face as I was expecting to see Anthony's name on my screen. Disappointment and confusion replaced that excitement when I saw the unknown number that was lighting up my screen.

> Wassup Kyrah. This Jesse. I hope you had a good break. I was hoping we could meet up and catch up sometime. Hit me up. I'll see you around.

Jesse?? I rolled my eyes and ignored the message. I didn't know why he was texting me nor did I care to find out. After reading that message, I became so caught up in my thoughts and trying to distract myself that I almost missed Anthony's call. I took a deep breath before answering.

"Hey!" I answered as cheerfully as possible.

"Hey, beautiful. You busy?"

"No, sir. I was actually waiting for you to call me. What's up?"

It's almost like I could hear his beautiful smile through the phone. He chuckled lightly.

"Good. I got a surprise for you. Meet me at my room in like ten minutes."

Butterflies filled my stomach. I wondered and tried to internally guess what the surprise was. I said "Okay", and we hung up.

I had ten minutes to get decent before I had to be downstairs in his room. I decided to throw on some leggings, an oversized sweatshirt that was cut to hang off the shoulders, and my comfy furry house boots. Ten minutes later I was standing outside of Anthony's door. I lightly knocked and waited for someone to answer. The door opened and Anthony's face appeared with a smile.

"Hey, babygirl. Come in." He stepped to the side, and I walked into his suite completely confused. There was a small lit-up Christmas tree on their side table by the couch with two small boxes under it. I looked at Anthony and squinted in curiosity.

"Anthony... What's going on here?" He smirked and walked towards the tree. He picked up the two boxes and handed them to me.

I gasped lightly, "Anthony, what? —" He shook his head.

"Just open it", he said watching me intently. I exhaled and began opening the box that read "this one first". Inside was a beautiful charm bracelet that had a charm the shape of a heart. I looked closely at the charm and noticed that it read "A&K".

"Oh, Anthony! This is beautiful. Thank you", I said looking at him with glossy eyes. He moved closer, closing the gap between us.

"Open the other one," he said. I put the first box down and then opened the next one. Inside was a mistletoe and I chuckled.

"Really?" I asked laughing harder. He laughed with me and gently grabbed my waist. He took the mistletoe from me and held it over our heads.

"I believe you owe me a kiss," he said with a smirk. He began leaning his head down so his lips could meet mine. I gave a small smile.

"I guess so," I responded almost in a whisper. Seconds later his lips touched mine ever so softly and I instantly melted. His arm that was holding up the mistletoe dropped, and he wrapped both his arms around my waist. I moved in closer and deepened the kiss. A low grunt escaped his throat, and I smiled a little. Suddenly he broke the kiss and looked down with a smirk. He bit his bottom lip as he met my gaze.

"Boundaries remember?" he joked. I chuckled.

"You're right... Thank you for this, though. I really appreciate it... all of it." He gently kissed me on the forehead.

"Merry Christmas, Kyrah."

I smiled, "Merry Christmas, Anthony."

Since it was getting late and we were trying our hands at this whole boundary idea, I decided to head back to my room for the night. Knowing it was Sunday evening made me realize that classes started back up tomorrow, and I was not looking forward to it. However, I refused to have another semester like the last one, so I was going to change my attitude about it. Before I went to bed, I decided to write out my new class schedule on my calendar and place it on my wall where I could see it. Feeling inspired, I also went ahead and organized my desk and wrote out a few Bible verses that I felt would keep me going. After finishing everything, I took a deep breath and stared at myself in my mirror.

"Okay, Kyrah. This semester will be better. Just stay focused and connected to God. Don't get caught up. Just do your work and pass. Do your best and you'll be fine." I smiled to myself happy to see the familiar woman in the mirror. It had been a long time since I was able to look at myself and like what I saw. But something about tonight was different. Perhaps I'd finally found my new confidence after finally starting my healing process.

After a few more moments of smiling at myself, sleep began to take over and I couldn't stand it any longer. I changed into my pajamas and climbed into my bed. I closed my eyes and took a deep breath. Suddenly, a simple prayer fell from my lips.

"God, please give me the strength to make it through this semester. And keep me close to you. In Jesus's name, amen."

Chapter Sixteen

The next morning, I woke up refreshed and ready to tackle the day. I picked up my phone to check the time. 8:00. I had exactly two hours before my first class for the day. I decided to go ahead and get up so I could shower and get ready. As I was putting the final touches on my outfit, my phone rang.

"Hey, Anthony", I answered after putting my phone on speaker so I could put my shoes on.

"Hey, good morning. What time is your class?" he asked sounding a little breathy.

"It's at 10. I was just getting dressed so I wouldn't lollygag. I was actually about to head to the caf to grab some breakfast. You wanna come—" A sudden knock on the main door interrupted me before I could finish. "Hold on, Anthony" came from my lips as I placed the phone down on my bed and headed towards the door. To my surprise, Anthony was standing on the other side. He hung up the phone and smiled. I returned the smile.

"Yes, I would love to go to breakfast with you," he finally responded.

I laughed, "Okay, just let me grab my bag and stuff." Thank God I'd ordered my books ahead of time since my professors had emailed the syllabi two weeks in advance. I headed back to my room and grabbed my bag, my phone, and keys. I closed my door, and we headed out of the suite.

Breakfast with Anthony was just what I needed before heading to my classes. Last semester I slacked off because I was dealing with so much. But this semester, I was determined to get back on it. I made it a goal to stay on top of my work and remember why I was at school in the first place. This first week back was the beginning of getting back to my life after everything that happened with Jesse. And honestly, I was ready to forgive him fully so I could live my life. I also wanted to enjoy the little bit of time I had left with Anthony since this was his last semester before he graduated.

Around 8:00 pm, I'd finally finished up my last class for the day. I was walking back to my suite when I noticed Jesse sitting outside my building talking on the phone. Anxiety started to build up in my chest. I wanted to walk the opposite way before he noticed me. *Okay, Kyrah... Take a deep breath. It's okay. You can do this. Just keep walking.* After gathering my thoughts, I began to take slower steps towards the entrance. As I was getting closer, he looked up and stopped talking on the phone. He slowly pulled the phone away from his ear and stared at me. I froze meeting his gaze.

"Kyrah? Hey..." he said somewhat lowly.

"Um... Hey..." I responded. We stared at each other awkwardly before I'd had enough and broke eye contact. My feet started moving again and I walked inside the building heading to the front desk to swipe my ID. Suddenly I heard his voice calling out my name.

"Kyrah! Wait up!" He caught up to me trying to catch his breath. I turned around and just looked at him, not responding.

"Um... I know we've already talked everything out, but I was wondering if you wanted to meet sometime and catch up. I really miss you, Ky..."

Those were the words I wanted to hear months ago, but now I cringed at the thought of them. Why couldn't he understand that we had nothing more to talk about? I sighed and shook my head.

"Jesse... Look, I-"

"Just... Just consider it before saying 'no'. Please?" I shook my head feeling myself giving in. Part of me felt bad for him because he really looked desperate to get back into my good graces. But at this point, I just wanted to be done with him altogether.

"Okay, Jesse. This is not a 'yes' ... But it's also not a 'no'. Just give me some time, please, okay?"

He quickly smiled and exhaled.

"Yeah, yeah! Sure, no problem. I'll hit you up," he finally responded.

I nodded, "Yeah... sure... I gotta go. I'll see you around." I quickly walked away before he could respond. I swiped my card and practically raced upstairs to my suite. Tamra and Raynah were both sitting in the living room on the couch talking. They greeted me as I placed my books and bag down in one of the chairs. They saw the annoyed expression on my face as I sat down. Tamra frowned in concern.

"What's wrong?" she asked.

I shook my head replaying the conversation with Jesse. I couldn't believe I actually gave him the time of day, but maybe this was my way of finally forgiving him.

"Nothing... I just saw Jesse and he asked me to meet up with him to catch up because he misses me." Simultaneously, they both rolled their eyes. I told them the conversation and that I didn't deny nor accept his invitation. Both looked at me confused.

"Wait... Why didn't you just say 'no'? He's put you through enough," Raynah replied.

I shrugged. "I wish I could tell you. I just felt kinda bad for him because he seemed sincere. I don't want to meet up with him, but I am also curious to hear what he has to say."

"Mhm," Tamra started, "And what will Anthony have to say?" I rolled my eyes. At this point, I was tired of caring what anybody had to say or thought about my decisions.

"Honestly, I love him, but I don't care. I'm tired of considering how Anthony or Jesse feel about my decisions. If we wanna be real, they both hurt me, Anthony just so happens to have actually understood how he hurt me and made the necessary changes. But if I wanna go hang out with Jesse, I will. Anthony is not my boyfriend, and he doesn't dictate my life. I've been through enough. I've put my life on hold and went against my own morals for both of them. I'm tired. I just had the worst few months of my life and I'm finally moving on from it. I refuse to keep making decisions based on how a dude feels. I'm getting my life back together. I'm focusing on myself. So, maybe I will meet up with Jesse to catch up. Maybe I won't. But whatever decision I make will be because I made the decision. Not Anthony, not Jesse, not anybody else."

Finally taking a breath, I closed my eyes for a second, silently applauding myself for standing up for myself for once. After I opened my eyes, I noticed my friends looking at me with smiles on their faces.

"There's our girl", Raynah said.

"Yep. She's back," Tamra added. I laughed and sighed.

"And it feels good to be back."

Chapter Seventeen

A few days had passed, and I'd been so focused on getting my schoolwork done to raise my GPA back up. I was also distracting myself so I wouldn't have to decide about meeting up with Jesse. I was wrestling with the possible outcome of meeting up with him or denying his invitation.

Shaking those thoughts out of my head, I continued writing my paper in the library that was due Sunday. I was starting to feel like my old self and that was making me happy. Music was playing softly in my right ear as I was zoning back into my work.

Suddenly I heard a low deep voice ask, "Excuse me, is this seat taken?"

Without looking in the person's direction, I responded, "No, just let me get my stuff."

I grabbed my stuff, still not looking at the mysterious person. I heard a deep chuckle as he sat down beside me.

"So, you just not gon' look at me?" he said. I looked up and saw Anthony sitting beside me. I laughed.

"My bad. I'm writing a paper." He smirked. My insides melted as he looked into my eyes. His hair was pulled back into a low ponytail showing off his perfectly structured face. He noticed me staring at him and chuckled. He turned his gaze to my laptop looking at my work.

"What you writin' about?" I followed his gaze looking back at my work. My shoulders slouched as I briefly gave him an overview of the assignment. He nodded as he kept reading the prompt that I handed him.

"You need some help?" I smiled nervously scrunching my nose.

"If you don't mind?"

He smiled, "Nah, I gotchu."

We sat in the library for a few hours going over the assignment numerous times to make sure it was done right. He would check what I wrote after I finished a section. Once 9:00 rolled around, we both decided that it was time to call it a night.

"A'ight, we'll get some more done tomorrow," he said as he helped me pack my stuff.

"Okay. Thank you, again. I really appreciate it. I owe you big." He stopped and stared at me.

"Come to dinner with me and we'll call it even." My face burned with blush, and I nodded.

"Deal."

We found a nice 24-hour Diner that was not too far from campus. As we waited for our food, we made small talk. I wrestled with telling him about Jesse because I honestly didn't feel like getting into all of that. But he's become one of my best friends and I just really wanted him to know. Out of everybody I talk to these days, I feel like I can be the most vulnerable with him. At this point, he knows me more than anybody.

"What's on your mind?" he asked as I got silent and stared mindlessly at the dessert menu. I rolled my eyes playfully.

"What?"

He chuckled, "You slouch your shoulders when you're about to have a panic attack or you're overthinking." I froze before taking a deep breath.

"I didn't know you noticed that..." I finally replied.

He bit his bottom lip slightly as he looked into my eyes making my stomach knot up.

"I notice everything about you..."

I blushed as I looked into his eyes. I don't know what it was about this man, but he had me. I couldn't shake him even if I wanted to. He just got me like no one else could. I was falling in deep for him and I would be lying if I said I didn't like it.

"Well, to answer your question... I saw Jesse the other day."

His demeanor was calm... so calm and reassuring that all my anxiety melted away.

"How did that go?" he asked genuinely.

I shrugged. "He wants to hang out. He texted me when I first got back from break, but I ignored him. He just wants to talk. Says he misses me." He nodded his head slowly, choosing his words carefully.

"How do you feel about that?"

I shook my head, "I honestly don't know. I'm conflicted. Do I go and hear him out? Or just dead the whole thing? Because we honestly have nothing else to talk about. I don't miss him. I don't really want to be around him... I'm finally starting to feel like myself. I'm focusing on me, getting my schoolwork done so I can raise my GPA back up... So, I really don't need the distraction. I just don't know what to do..."

He cleared his throat and looked deep into my eyes.

"You should hear him out." I frowned not expecting him to say that. He read my facial expression and put his hands up to stop me from protesting. I pouted and waited for him to explain. He continued, "Just hear the man out. You heard me out. I'm not saying go be best friends with him like we are, now. And I know he hurt you. But I hurt you, too. I may not have hurt you the same way, but you were hurt in the end in both situations. Not that he deserves it, but you deserve to at least get that closure. So, don't do it for him... Do it for you."

He was right. I needed to hear Jesse out for my own peace of mind. There were still moments where I would find myself with tears in my eyes wondering what I did to deserve that much pain. It didn't seem fair. But I didn't have the answers. No, I don't think I deserved it at all, but I was still curious to hear what he'd been wanting to tell me all these months.

"Okay. I'll do it," I agreed.

We enjoyed the rest of our dinner and didn't get back to campus until around 11:30. Once he walked me to my suite, I passed out exhausted from the long hours of studying and writing the paper.

As promised, we met up again the next day in the library to finish working on the paper. He watched me submit it online as I sighed in relief.

"Thank you so much for helping me. I know it wasn't due until tomorrow but I'm so glad to already be done with it."

He smiled, "No problem, beautiful." We spent the rest of the day together since he had the day off. It was nice to be around him in this way. I couldn't help but wonder if we would be taking it to the next step in our relationship any time soon. We both wanted to take it slow, so there was no rush. But I couldn't lie, my heart felt ready.

As I was lying in my bed after Anthony left, I decided to text Jesse. I inhaled and held my breath before pressing send. After contemplating what to say, I just typed what I felt.

After I hit send, I exhaled, put my phone on DND, and drifted off to sleep.

Chapter Eighteen

I woke up the next morning refreshed and ready to start my day. Thanks to Anthony's help, I didn't have to worry about my paper, so I really had the entire day to relax. I checked my phone and saw that Jesse agreed to meet in the cafeteria at 2. Although I was dreading this conversation, it was necessary, and I just needed to get it over with. There was no need to put off the inevitable. But until then, I decided to go to church. Anthony had to work this morning so I would be going by myself. I hadn't been going consistently, but I was working on it. Plus, I really wanted to see Moriah since I hadn't talked to her in a while.

As I was getting ready to hop in the shower, I heard my text tone ring and I checked to see who it was.

> Morning gorgeous. I hope you have a good day. I pray the conversation between you and Jesse answers all your questions and starts your healing. I'll hit you, later.

I quickly replied to Anthony's message and hopped in the shower. Once I finished, I put some clothes on, refreshed my curls, and put on some mascara and lip gloss. I grabbed my keys, purse, and phone and headed out of the door.

Church was a good distraction that I needed to get my mind off this meet-up. It ended at exactly 1:30 so that would give me thirty minutes to hurry and get to the cafeteria. I prayed the entire drive back to campus.

"Lord," I began, "I'm leaving the outcome of this conversation to you. I ask that you soften my heart and open me up to total forgiveness. I don't wanna do this... But I know I need to. I just need you throughout all of this..."

I sighed as I pulled into a parking spot. I didn't have time to go to my room to change into something more comfortable, so I just headed straight there. As I was praying while walking, I could feel the peace of God take over my body and I knew I was ready. No matter what, God already had it under control and there was nothing I could do besides show up. I was ready.

My eyes searched for Jesse as I walked into the cafeteria. I didn't see him, so I decided to just grab a slice of pizza and sit down while I waited for him. Before I could take a bite, I heard his voice call out my name. I looked up and saw him walking towards me. I took a deep breath and mustered up a small smile to greet him.

"Hey," he said approaching me and sitting down.

"Hi", I responded.

He sighed and looked at me sincerely. "Thanks for meeting up with me. I know I'm the last person you want to see, but I appreciate you coming."

I nodded, "Well, I'm here and I actually want to hear what you have to say... So, what's up?"

Unsurprised by my blunt response, he proceeded.

"Kyrah... I am so sorry. We already talked about how I cheated on you multiple times... mostly during the summer when we were apart." *Ouch*. I took a deep breath before responding. I took a few seconds to think and choose my words wisely so this conversation wouldn't go left, but I could start to feel the anxiety and the tears coming. *Don't do it for him... Do it for you.* I could hear Anthony's reassuring voice in the back of my mind replaying everything he said yesterday. I looked at Jesse with calm eyes and spoke in a calm tone.

"Can I ask you why? I just want to know what I did to deserve that..." was all I could say.

He shook his head, "Nothin'. You didn't deserve that..."

"So, why??"

"Because we were missing that physical connection. We would always come so close and then you would change your mind. So, I just went to find it elsewhere... And that wasn't fair to you. You're allowed to change your mind about sex. But I should've just ended things before it even got that far. As much as I wanted to wait with you and commit to it, I was weak. I'm too weak for that kinda commitment."

I nodded allowing myself to process everything. I didn't try to force a response or rush myself to reply. Instead, I had a silent conversation with God, asking Him to help me. And at that very moment, I decided to forgive him and let it go.

"You know, Jesse... I understand. We just weren't a match for each other. I hate that things had to end the way they did, but we can't go back and change it. But I do want you to know how much I was hurt... You don't understand what all of this did to me. I'd never experienced that kind of depression before. And it wasn't because we broke up, but it was more so because I was confused about how all of this was happening to me just as I was starting to feel happy. But I realize I made a mistake. I made the mistake of making you my happiness and looking to you to fill a role that only God can fill. And when you couldn't meet those expectations, I crumbled. That's what hurt the most. I'm not excusing anything you did at all... but I do see how I allowed myself to be so blinded by my expectations that I couldn't see the reality that was right before my eyes... However, it was a learning experience for me. As strange as it sounds, I needed this to happen so I could learn to love myself again and get back to taking care of myself without caring about what anyone else thinks or what anybody has to say... So, I forgive you. Not for you, but for me. I just want to move on and leave all of this behind."

Jesse looked at me with a stunned expression. I'm sure he expected me to go off and give him a piece of my mind. Honestly, I thought I would do that, too. But I was at peace... All I could feel was peace. Everything that happened to me in the past year didn't matter anymore. The hurt and pain caused by Anthony and Jesse faded away in that moment. I looked at him and gave him a small reassuring smile. He returned the smile.

"I, uh... thanks, Kyrah. That means a lot." I nodded. I looked at my phone and saw what time it was. Although this conversation was going well, I didn't want to make small talk. I had somewhere I needed to be. I looked at Jesse and smiled.

"Thanks for inviting me to lunch. This was a much-needed conversation. I actually have to go." He nodded.

"No problem. Thanks for meeting me. I really appreciate it."

I stood up gathering my empty plate and belongings.

"See you 'round, Jesse."

"See you, Kyrah." I hurriedly put my plate away and sped walk to our building. Before walking inside, I decided to call Anthony. The phone rang for what felt like forever until he finally picked up.

"What's up, beautiful?" he said through the phone.

"Hey, are you on campus?"

"I'm actually pulling in the parking lot now."

"Okay, stay there." I hung up before he could respond and almost ran to meet him in the parking lot. I scanned the lot looking for his car. Once I spotted him, I ran over to him. He got out of the car and gave me a puzzled look. I stood in front of him trying to catch my breath.

"Hey, you good?" he asked with concern in his voice. I walked closer to him, grabbed a handful of locs, guiding his head down until his lips met mine. Without hesitation, he wrapped his strong arms around my waist, pulling me closer to him. I deepened the kiss not to bring up any sexual tension but to finally express my true feelings for him. I couldn't keep them to myself anymore. Keeping all these feelings bottled up was becoming too overwhelming for me... it was time for him to know.

We finally parted both trying to catch our breath. He stared at me with so much love and I couldn't help but melt. He smiled that million-dollar smile that I love oh so much.

"Where did that come from?", he asked with a chuckle.

"Anthony..." I took a step back so I could look him deep in his eyes. I smiled. "I love you. I'm in love with you. And that's never going to change. It's you. It's always been you."

He exhaled and his smile grew bigger, "I love you so much, Kyrah." He pulled me back into his embrace and kissed me tenderly.

Chapter Nineteen

"**B**abe, you look. I'm too scared," I told Anthony as we were checking our grades. It was the end of the semester, so our final grades were finally posted. I'd been working overtime to get my GPA back up, but I was terrified to see if all my hard work had paid off.

Anthony laughed and put one arm around my waist as we were sitting on the same side in the same booth in the campus coffee house where we first saw each other this school year. He placed his free hand under my chin making me look at him.

"Hey," he started as he looked me in my eyes, "No matter what, I'm proud of you. I've never seen anyone get back up the way you did. Anybody else would've quit. So, pat yourself on the back just for not giving up and kicking ass—forgive me, Lord—despite everything you went through."

I smiled, "Thank you... I still want you to look, though." He laughed and rolled his eyes. After a few moments of silence, I became impatient. The anxiety was getting to me, and my hands started sweating.

"Well," he started before taking a long pause. I look at him, annoyed by his dramatics.

"Babe, come on."

He laughed, "Baby... You did that. Take a look." *3.24?? 3 A's and 1 B???* A huge smile grew on my face as I exhaled in relief. I couldn't believe I pulled that off. Proud wasn't even the word. I shook my head in disbelief. After the long and all-around tough semester I'd had, I really didn't think I'd be able to do it. But I'm so glad I did. This was an accomplishment I hope to be able to encourage my kids with one day.

"I can't believe I actually pulled that off," I finally responded still staring at the screen. I turned my gaze to Anthony who was looking at me with a proud smile.

"I knew you could. I told you you're a nerd." I rolled my eyes and lightly hit him on his shoulder. He laughed.

"I'm serious," he continued, "the first night we met, you were studying and there was a whole party going on. I was like 'Nah, this girl is different'", he finished. I gave him a small smile.

"You still remember that, huh?"

He inched his face closer to mine and bit his bottom lip slightly. I blushed as I got lost in his eyes.

"Of course, I do. The night I met the woman of my dreams." He kissed me sweetly.

"I love you," I said after our lips parted.

"I love you," he replied with a small grin.

Later that evening I decided to start packing my room up. As excited as I was about finishing off this school year on a strong note, I was slightly sad that this was Anthony's last year at this school. Graduation was in three days, and I was so proud of him for making it this far. I also couldn't wait to finally meet his family even though I was nervous. He'd spent the last few days telling me all about them and it made me excited to meet the people that watched him grow up, the people I'd heard so much about. I just knew that they were as proud as I am of him.

As I was packing up my clothes that were hanging in my closet, Tamra lightly knocked on my open door as she peeked in. I gave her a big smile and invited her in. She sighed.

"Man," she began, "another year down… That's crazy." I looked at her and put my hands on my hips. I exhaled deeply.

"You're telling me," I began responding. "I can't believe this year is already over. The first semester seemed to drag, but this semester had somewhere to be, huh?"

She laughed, "I guess so, girl. Are you excited to go see Anthony walk across the stage?" I blushed as I pictured him in his cap and gown.

"Definitely. I am so proud of him."

She nodded, "Aren't you going to miss him?" I thought about it for a second and shrugged.

"Yeah, of course… But we both knew this day was coming. I'm just glad he lives nearby so I'll still see him. We're already planning to spend the majority of the summer together since I've decided to take summer classes."

She nodded, "That's true. Well, I'm pretty much done with my packing. You need any help?" I put up my prayer hands.

"Oh my gosh, yes. I was in here getting overwhelmed. I would greatly appreciate the help." She laughed.

"I gotchu, girl."

We started going through my things and in that moment, I decided to purge a lot of things by throwing away old journals, old schoolwork that I knew I wouldn't need, and bagging some old clothes that I hadn't worn in ages. It was just time to start fresh since I felt I was entering a new season in my life.

As this school year ended, I was very thankful to God for getting me through. There was no way I would've gotten through it on my own. There were so many moments where I just wanted to give up. But God showed up. Like he always does.

After three long hours of going through my things, Tamra and I were finally finished, and I was pretty much all packed up. All that was left were the things I planned to wear for the next few days, including tonight. Anthony and I made plans to go on one last date. He would be working the next few days since he took the day of his graduation off (of course). He told me to dress fancy, so I had to dig deep for an outfit. Tamra helped me find the perfect dress and the perfect shoes to match: A light brown backless dress with nude-heeled sandals. I took my time getting ready. For some reason, I really wanted to "wow" him. After I took a long hot shower, I pampered myself by polishing my toes and my nails. I styled my hair by defining the curls in my afro. I put on pearl studs in my ears, and a gold necklace, and did some light makeup with nude glossy lips. Once I slipped my dress and shoes on, I looked at myself in the mirror and smiled.

"You look beautiful," I told myself. Before I knew it, it was 8:00 and Anthony was knocking on my room door. I'd heard him come in the suite but thank God he and Tamra were talking for a few minutes so I could finish getting ready. I took a deep breath and opened the door to find him standing there looking like the most handsome man in the world. He looked up and smiled at me.

"Kyrah... Wow." *Bingo.* "You look stunning, babygirl... I'm blown away." He grabbed my hand lightly and spun me around. "And she got the back out??? Oh Lawd!" he exaggerated.

I laughed, "Wow to you, too, sir. You look incredible. I've seen you dress up but not like this." His locs were in a half-up-half-down style with a bun and the rest flowing down to the middle of his back with his fresh line-up. He wore a burnt orange shirt with a long tan cardigan and some brown slacks that were rolled up a little to show off his ankles and nice shoes. My favorite part was his glasses. After spending the next five minutes staring and complimenting each other, we finally headed out.

The ride to the restaurant was so relaxing. All we did was talk while he held my hand. I looked out of the window and took in the beautiful sight of the Atlanta city lights. As we approached the nice restaurant, I smiled. He parked the car and hurried over to open my car door. We walked inside holding hands and waited to speak to the hostess.

"Hi, welcome!", she greeted us with a big smile.

Anthony smiled, "Hi, reservations for Wright." She checked the screen in front of her and smiled when she spotted his last name. She grabbed two menus and stepped from behind the host stand.

"You two can follow me right this way", she said before she led us to our table. "You two enjoy your evening." Leaving us alone, we both looked over our menus.

"Get whatever you want, baby", Anthony said as he continued looking over his menu. I looked at him and chuckled.

"You always spoil me." He met my gaze and smiled.

"And I always will."

The rest of dinner was filled with laughter and just all-around great conversation. I was so glad that we were able to reconnect this school year. After everything that happened between us last year, I wasn't sure if we'd even talk ever again. But I'm glad I was wrong. One of the main things I learned this year was that despite everything I go through, God is always with me. And ironically, he used Anthony to show me that.

God used him to remind me that I was never alone. God was always there comforting me even in my darkest moments just like Anthony was. And I was forever grateful for that.

We rode back to campus holding hands just like we used to. He walked me back to my room one last time before I moved out tomorrow and stood in front of me with a small smile.

"This is it, huh?" he said with a hint of sadness in his voice.

"I guess so... It's gonna be so weird next year without you here", I admitted. He nodded in silence and looked down at his feet. I gently held the sides of his face making him look at me. I smiled.

"But I'm so proud of you. I can't wait to see you walk across that stage." He smirked and wrapped his arms around my waist. He leaned his head down and lightly kissed me on the lips. I smiled.

"I love you,", he said lowly.

"I love you, too."

Chapter Twenty

"**A**nthony Jamal Wright" the dean announced loudly into the microphone. A wave of applause and cheer grew as I watched him walk across the stage. I smiled to myself and clapped like the proud girlfriend I was.

"Bachelor of Business Management with a Concentration in Human Resource Management. Anthony is graduating *cum laude* with a 3.79 GPA." The applause grew louder as we all cheered him on. Words could not express how proud of him I was. All the late-night study sessions and all-nighters while working a full-time internship were completely worth it and paid off in the end.

The rest of the graduation ceremony went by fast. Before I knew it, the final speaker was closing and congratulating the graduates one last time before they moved their tassels from one side to the other. After it was over, I raced outside to wait for Anthony with Tamra by my side. Butterflies entered my stomach as I began to think about the thought of meeting his family. After all this time, I'd never even been in the same room as them until today.

About ten full minutes passed before all the graduates came out of the door to meet their families. From afar, I spotted Anthony walking towards his family with a huge smile plastered on his face. I smiled to myself. He searched the crowd until his eyes landed on me. He walked over to me, and I took a deep breath.

"Hey," he said smiling down at me.

"Hey, you. Congratulations, my love."

"Thank you, beautiful." He leaned down and kissed me sweetly making me blush. He then turned his attention to Tamra and greeted her. They exchanged small talk for a second before he grabbed my hand.

"You mind if I steal her away?", he asked her. She shook her head no and smiled.

"Of course not. I'll catch up with you guys later. I gotta head back home."

"Okay, thanks for coming with me," I said as I gave her a big hug. We exchanged goodbyes and parted ways. I followed Anthony as he held my hand over to meet his family.

"Mom, Dad, this is Kyrah, my girlfriend." I blushed internally as I heard him say that. It felt as if it was my first time hearing it.

"Oh Kyrah, it's so nice to finally meet you, sweetie!" his mom exclaimed. She opened her arms and hugged me tightly as if she'd already known me. His dad smiled while giving me a big hug as well.

"We've heard so much about you, young lady." A smile grew on my face as I could feel myself start to relax. We all talked for a bit before deciding on where we were going for dinner.

"Okay, we'll meet you guys there," Anthony said before his parents left us alone.

"Ready?" he asked. I nodded. We walked to his car and headed right to the restaurant.

Dinner was so nice. His family welcomed me with no hesitation and was eager to get to know me. They asked me the basic questions and I gladly answered every single one. Throughout the dinner, they expressed how they couldn't wait to see me walk across that same stage in a few years. After this year, I honestly couldn't wait either. Seeing Anthony walk reminded me of how I could do it. And now that we're together again, I know that he will be with me every step of the way to help me and encourage me when I need it.

After dinner, I said my goodbyes to his family and hugged them one last time before we all parted ways. Anthony and I rode in his car to my hotel in silence but still holding hands. It was almost as if neither of us wanted to leave one another. Granted, I would be back for my summer classes but we both knew it wouldn't be the same. Without him living on campus, we would have to put in extra effort for each other and we both knew how that would either make or break us. Once we arrived at the hotel, we just sat in the car, enjoying each other's presence.

"Anthony," I said breaking the silence. I looked at him and he looked at me waiting for me to continue.

"What are you thinking?" I finally said. He sighed.

"Nothing... Just how everything is going to change. I know we'll be fine, but I'm still going to miss seeing you randomly on campus and coming up behind you and hugging you. It's just not going to be the same. Like, real life is really about to start for me. No more homework or campus parties," we laughed, "but I'm ready. And I'm glad out of all of this, you and I crossed paths." I held out my hand for him to hold. He gently grabbed my hand, intertwining our fingers together.

He was absolutely right. Everything was about to be different. Was I ready for that? I don't know. But I was now in a place where I just wanted to go with the flow and see how everything played out without trying to control it. We both knew that we were meant to be together.

At this point, it was just a matter of us intentionally working to keep our relationship going. And I was ready to do that.

"Hey...", I said as he looked at me, "you're gonna do great. I know you will."

He smirked, held my hand up to his lips, and kissed it so sweetly. After talking for a little while longer, he walked to my hotel room to make sure I got in safely. We stood outside of the door for a while just embracing each other.

"I'll see you later, okay? You be safe on the road tomorrow. Call me if you need to," he said while still holding me.

"I will. I love you," I said looking up at him.

"I love you," he responded. He leaned down and kissed me. We kissed as if we'd never get the chance to do it again. I broke it and chuckled.

"Boundaries, mister," I joked.

He smirked, "You right." He unwrapped his arms and opened the door for me before handing me the room key. I walked into the room.

"Goodnight, boyfriend," I said as I held the door open.

"Goodnight babygirl," he winked and walked away. I closed the door and exhaled. I got ready for bed fighting off the sad feeling of having to leave tomorrow. Getting in bed, I prayed, thanking God once again for getting me through another year. It was a long one, but I was thankful to see the other side of it.

I woke up the next morning bright and early ready to hit the road. Checking the room one last time, I made sure I had everything I'd brought for my overnight stay. I grabbed my packed bag, my purse, my phone, and the room key and headed downstairs. After checking out and packing up my car, I got on the driver's side and prepared for the trip home. A smile grew on my face as I put my car in reverse. I drove out of the parking lot and started making my way toward the interstate.

Another year down...

Epilogue

Two years later...

June 2018

I t was the day after my graduation, and I was getting dressed in my brand-new apartment. Hey baby, I'm almost there. I read my text message and responded with an "okay" while trying to hurry and finish getting ready. He said it was a special occasion and he wanted me to get somewhat dressed up. I don't know what this was about, but I was excited to see where he was taking me. He'd hinted that his family was doing something, and they wanted me to come so I couldn't say no. I had grown to really love them and wanted to spend so much time with them.

While I was putting my shoes on, I heard jiggling keys at my door and knew that it was Anthony unlocking the door. He walked in and called out for me.

"It's me, baby," he announced. I stood up and checked myself one last time in the mirror as I heard his footsteps getting closer. He stood at the door and smiled.

"You are just breathtaking," he said as he walked closer to me. He wrapped his arms around my waist making me blush.

"Thank you, handsome."

"You ready?" he asked. I nodded and smiled.

We headed out of the door after I grabbed my belongings. The drive to wherever seemed long. He stopped the car at a gas station and pulled out a blindfold.

"You gotta put this on," he said. I laughed.

"Anthony... I just know y'all are not tryna surprise me with a big party."

He laughed, "Daaaaang, something like that. Just put it on, baby." I playfully rolled my eyes and complied. He tied the blindfold on me and kept driving to wherever he was taking me. Before I knew it, we pulled up and he helped me out of the car. We walked into a building with soft live music playing as he held my hand guiding me inside. He took the blindfold off my eyes, and I noticed that he'd brought me to my favorite coffee shop. I noticed the lights were dimmer than usual and no one else was there. I frowned in confusion and looked at Anthony.

"Anthony, what in the world are we doing here?" I began with a small smile forming on my lips. "And are you sure they're open? Doesn't look like there's anyone else here," I said with a confused smirk. He bit his bottom lip and smirked.

"I rented out the place. It's just us." My mouth dropped instantly. He grabbed one of my hands and guided me further into the coffee shop and there I saw a single table for two. He pulled out my seat and I sat down. I watched him as he sat down, not even noticing the music being played on stage.

"Anthony... This is amazing. How did you do this? You know how much I love this place."

He nodded and smiled, "Yeah, that's why I did it. You love to come here, and I wanted to do something special for you just because." I blushed.

"That's very sweet." Soon after, one of the baristas came to our table and sat my regular order on the table in front of me and Anthony's regular order in front of him. We made small talk for a while, but something was off about him. He wasn't as talkative or joking around as he usually does. But I just went along with it because I just figured he had a lot on his mind. We both turned our attention to the singer and live band on the stage. Ironically, she was singing one of my favorite songs, New Balance by Jhene Aiko. I closed my eyes and listened to her sing those beautiful lyrics while humming along with her. This song spoke to me in many ways as it described the way I felt about Anthony.

Then suddenly, I opened my eyes and saw Anthony on the stage where the singer was supposed to be. The band kept playing lowly and Anthony grabbed the mic.

"Kyrah, do you remember when we met in the vending room? I have to tell you that you literally took my breath away from that very moment. After that night, I couldn't get you out of my mind. Every time I left my room, I was hoping that I would see you again so I could at least get your name. Then we bumped into each other, and I knocked all of your food out of your hands," he paused and chuckled. I laughed as tears fell from my eyes.

He continued, "I wish I could say I did that on purpose because I really wanted to know you, but I have to believe that that was God giving me a second chance to make my move. You have changed my life for the better. I will forever be thankful to God for bringing you into my life. I don't think you understand the impact you've had on me. You've made such an impact that I can't even see my life without you in it... And I don't want to..." He stopped, gave the mic back to the singer, and made his way off the stage. He walked towards me, and I could feel my heart about to beat out of my chest. He stood in front of me.

"Kyrah..." he started before he began kneeling in front of me. More tears spilled from my eyes, and I placed my hand over my mouth. He pulled out a ring box from his pocket and opened it. He looked me deep in my eyes, with tears in his. His deep voice cracked a little.

"Baby girl, I told you I would make this happen one day. This is me keeping my word. I am ready to take the next step with you. I am ready to live the rest of my life with you. Kyrah, will you marry me?"

I nodded so quickly as "yes" fell from my lips. I wrapped my arms around his neck and hugged him tight. He pulled away and slipped the beautiful diamond ring on my ring finger, then pulled me in for a kiss. Suddenly, I heard cheering and clapping coming from behind me and the lights were turned on. I turned around to find my friends, my family, and his family standing far behind us watching everything unfold...

To Be Continued

K armen Scott, a wife, and mother of two, is an Augusta, Georgia native. She received her high school diploma from Lucy Craft Laney High School in 2014 and her bachelor's degree in marketing from Brenau University in 2020. She is currently working towards her master's in clinical mental health counseling from Walden University. However, Karmen's first love is writing.

Karmen attended Georgia Gwinnett College from 2014-2017 where she wrote her very first novel, Inexperienced her freshman year. Although she wears many hats, writing will always be her passion. She is the founder of Child of Purpose, LLC and has a blog where she writes inspirational pieces to encourage her followers. Karmen hopes to continue her journey as a writer and published author in the years to come.

To learn more and follow her journey, visit www.childofpurpose blog.wordpress.com.

Read the first book of the Inexperienced Series:

Coming Soon...

INVITATION TO SALVATION

I know this is not usually something that is put at the
end of romance novels, but I am in a season where my
obedience is non-negotiable. And I will be honest and
say this is scary for me to do. But I have to do it.
With that, I want to say that if this is something that
doesn't interest you, I invite you to skim through or stop
here altogether. I promise you, I will not be offended.
However, I feel obligated to include this at the end of
my books, since all my written works are Christ centered,
and the heart of my writing is to shine light on who he is
and how he has moved in my life through my characters.
I am not here to beat you over the head with the Bible
or try to force my beliefs on anybody. This is merely me
just doing what I feel God is telling me to do.
So, if you have read this far and wish to continue, keep
reading. If this is not for you, I thank you for being here
and reading my book. I appreciate you from the bottom
of my heart. And in case you haven't heard it today, I
love you!

God's Word tells us in John 3:16 that He sent His one and
only Son to die on the cross at Calvary for our sins. The
entire world.

"For God so loved the world that He gave His only Begotten
Son, that whosoever believes in him shall not perish, but have
everlasting life."

Please know that despite everything that goes on in this
world, God is still God and He loves you. And if that's
something you can feel in your heart, please pray this
prayer with me:

Heavenly Father, thank you for sending your Son to die for
me. Please forgive me. I have made mistakes, but I believe
that through your Son and because of his perfect Sacrifice,
you have forgiven me for my sins. I confess that Jesus is Lord,
and I believe He died on the cross just for me and rose again
on the third day. I accept Jesus into my heart today and
choose to follow you.
In Jesus' Name, Amen.

I love you so much. And I pray that God continues to bless
you all the days of your life. May the Lord shine on you and
be gracious to you. May the Lord show you His favor and
give you His peace.